Grammar Guru

基礎文法寶典 ❸
Essential English Usage & Grammar

編著／J. B. Alter
審訂／劉美皇　呂香瑩

三民書局

Grammar Guru

國家圖書館出版品預行編目資料

Essential English Usage & Grammar 基礎文法寶典
／J. B. Alter編著;劉美皇,呂香瑩審訂.－－初版
一刷.－－臺北市: 三民，2008
　　冊；　公分

ISBN 978-957-14-5103-9　（平裝）

1. 英語 2.語法

805.16　　　　　　　　　　　　　　97018552

© Essential English Usage & Grammar 基礎文法寶典 3

編 著 者	J. B. Alter
審　　訂	劉美皇　呂香瑩
企劃編輯	王伊平
責任編輯	彭彥哲
美術設計	郭雅萍
發 行 人	劉振強
著作財產權人	三民書局股份有限公司
發 行 所	三民書局股份有限公司
	地址　臺北市復興北路386號
	電話　(02)25006600
	郵撥帳號　0009998-5
門 市 部	(復北店) 臺北市復興北路386號
	(重南店) 臺北市重慶南路一段61號
出版日期	初版一刷　2008年11月
編　　號	S 807520

行政院新聞局登記證局版臺業字第○二○○號

有著作權‧不准侵害

ISBN　978-957-14-5103-9　（平裝）

http://www.sanmin.com.tw　三民網路書店
※本書如有缺頁、破損或裝訂錯誤，請寄回本公司更換。

序

如果說，單字是英文的血肉，文法就是英文的骨架。想要打好英文基礎，兩者實應相輔相成，缺一不可。

只是，單字可以死背，文法卻不然。

學習文法，如果沒有良師諄諄善誘，沒有好書細細剖析，只落得個見樹不見林，徒然勞心費力，實在可惜。

Guru 原義指的是精通於某領域的「達人」，因此，這一套「文法 Guru」系列叢書，本著 Guru「導師」的精神，要告訴您：親愛的，我把英文文法變簡單了！

「文法 Guru」系列，適用對象廣泛，從初習英文的超級新鮮人、被文法糾纏得寢食難安的中學生，到鎮日把玩英文的專業行家，都能在這一套系列叢書中找到最適合自己的夥伴。

深願「文法 Guru」系列，能成為您最好的學習夥伴，伴您一同輕鬆悠遊英文學習的美妙世界。

有了「文法 Guru」，文法輕鬆上路！

前言

　　「**基礎文法寶典**」一套五冊，是專為中學生與一般社會大眾所設計，作為基礎課程教材或是課外自學之用。

　　英語教師往往對結構、句型、語法等為主的教學模式再熟悉不過。然而，現在學界普遍意識到**文法在語言學習的過程中亦佔有一席之地**，少了文法這一環，英語教學便顯得空洞。有鑑於此，市場上漸漸興起一股「**功能性文法**」的風潮。功能性文法旨在列舉用法並協助讀者熟悉文法專有名詞，而後者便是用以解釋及界定一語言各種功能的利器。

　　本套書各冊內容編排詳盡，涵蓋所有用法及文法要點；除此之外，本套書最強調的便是從不斷的練習中學好英文。每章所附的練習題皆經特別設計，提供讀者豐富多元的演練題型，舉凡**完成** (completion)、**修正** (modification)、**轉換** (conversion)、**合併** (integration)、**重述** (restatement)、**改寫** (alteration)、**變形** (transformation) 及**代換** (transposition)，應有盡有。

　　熟讀此書，將可幫助您完全理解各種文法及正確的表達方式，讓您在課業學習或日常生活上的英文程度突飛猛進。

給讀者的話

本書一套共五本，共分為二十一章，從最基礎的各式詞類介紹，一直到動詞的進階應用、基本書寫概念等，涵蓋所有的基本文法要義，為您建立一個完整的自修體系，並以豐富多樣的練習題為最大特色。

本書的主要細部單元包括：

USAGE PRACTICE→每個文法條目說明之下，皆有大量的例句或用法實例，讓您充分了解該文法規則之實際應用方式。

注意→很多文法規則皆有特殊的應用，或者是因應不同情境而產生相關變化，這些我們都以較小字的提示，列在本單元中。

但是我們會用→文法規則的例外情況也不少，我們在這單元直接以舉例的方式，說明這些不依循規則的情況。

小練習→每節介紹後，會有針對該節內容所設計的一段習題，可讓您即時驗證前面所學的內容。

應用練習→每章的內容結束後，我們都提供了非常充分的應用練習，而且題型豐富，各有其學習功能。建議您不要急於在短時間內將練習做完，而是漸進式地逐步完成，這樣可達成更好的學習效果。

本書文法內容完善，習題亦兼具廣度與深度，是您自修學習之最佳選擇，也可作為文法疑難的查閱參考，值得您細細研讀，慢慢體會。

基礎文法寶典 ❸
Essential English Usage & Grammar

目次

基礎文法寶典 ❸
Essential English Usage & Grammar

Chapter 10 時　態

10-1 現在簡單式

(a) 現在簡單式的否定句和疑問句必須使用助動詞 do 或 does。

USAGE PRACTICE		
肯定句	否定句	疑問句
▶ I **go**. 我去。	→ I **don't go**. 我不去。	→ **Do** I **go**? 我去嗎？
▶ We **go**. 我們去。	→ We **don't go**. 我們不去。	→ **Do** we **go**? 我們去嗎？
▶ They **go**. 他們去。	→ They **don't go**. 他們不去。	→ **Do** they **go**? 他們去嗎？
▶ He **goes**. 他去。	→ He **doesn't go**. 他不去。	→ **Does** he **go**? 他去嗎？
▶ She **goes**. 她去。	→ She **doesn't go**. 她不去。	→ **Does** she **go**? 她去嗎？
▶ It **goes**. 它去。	→ It **doesn't go**. 它不去。	→ **Does** it **go**? 它去嗎？
▶ I **want** to go. 我想去。	→ I **don't want** to go. 我不想去。	→ **Do** I **want** to go? 我想去嗎？
▶ He **uses** it. 他使用它。	→ He **doesn't use** it. 他不使用它。	→ **Does** he **use** it? 他使用它嗎？
▶ She **likes** cats. 她喜歡貓。	→ She **doesn't like** cats. 她不喜歡貓。	→ **Does** she **like** cats? 她喜歡貓嗎？

(b) 現在簡單式常和 usually、always、often、never、sometimes、generally、every day、once a week 等跟頻率相關的副詞或副詞片語連用，表示「現在習慣性的動作」。

USAGE PRACTICE
▶ I usually **drink** milk and **eat** bread in the morning.　我通常早上喝牛奶和吃麵包。
▶ They usually **walk** up this way.　他們經常沿著這條路走。
▶ He usually **goes** to his friend's house in the evening.　他經常在晚上去朋友的家。
▶ She always **sits** in that chair.　她總是坐在那張椅子上。

▶ My father always **smokes** a pipe after dinner. 我父親晚飯後總要抽菸斗。

▶ I always **do** my homework in the room. 我總是在這房間裡做功課。

▶ She always **takes** a bus to work. 她總是搭公車去工作。

▶ We often **sleep** in the afternoon. 我們常常睡午覺。

▶ He often **comes** late to school. 他上學經常遲到。

▶ They often **play** football together. 他們經常一起玩美式足球。

▶ He never **drinks** beer. 他從來不喝啤酒。

▶ That dog **doesn't have** a bath every day. 那隻狗沒有每天洗澡。

▶ I **walk** to school every day. 我每天走路上學。

▶ He **drives** to work every morning. 他每天早上開車去上班。

▶ We **go** to bed at ten every night. 我們每天晚上十點就寢。

▶ She **teaches** French three times a week. 她一週教法文課三次。

▶ They **wear** ties to school on Mondays. 他們每星期一打領帶去上學。

(c) 現在簡單式可以用來陳述一般性的真理、事實或格言。

USAGE PRACTICE

▶ Mount Everest **is** the highest mountain in the world. 埃佛勒斯峰是世界上最高的山峰。

▶ Tigers **roar**; they **do not bark**. 老虎是用吼的；不是吠叫。

▶ Mosquitoes **are** insects. 蚊子是昆蟲。

▶ Many trees **lose** their leaves in autumn. 許多樹在秋天會掉葉子。

▶ The sun **rises** in the east and **sets** in the west. 太陽從東方升起，從西方落下。

▶ The moon **goes** around the earth while the earth itself **revolves** around the sun.

月亮繞地球運行，而地球本身繞太陽旋轉。

▶ It often **rains** at this time of the year. 每年這個時候常下雨。

▶ Light **moves** faster than sound. 光速比音速快。

▶ Metals **expand** when heated. 金屬遇熱會膨脹。

▶ Mary **is** a girl's name. 瑪麗是女孩子的名字。

▶ Man **uses** his intelligence to create things. 人類使用智慧創造東西。

▶ Exchange **is** no robbery. 一個願打，一個願挨。

現在簡單式也可以用來引述引言或諺語。

▶ Blake **begins** the poem with the words, "Piping down the valleys wild...."
布萊克以這些字做為詩的開頭:「沿著渺無人煙的山谷吹奏著笛子…。」

▶ There is a proverb which **states** that too many cooks spoil the broth. 有個諺語説人多手雜。

(d) 在 when、as soon as、until、if 或 unless 等連接詞引導的副詞子句中,通常用現在簡單式代替未來式。

USAGE PRACTICE

▶ When the conductor **blows** his whistle, the train will start to move.
當車掌吹哨子,火車就會開始動。

▶ When the rain **stops**, walk to the shop with me. 當雨停的時候,跟我一起走去那家店。

▶ When he **returns**, he will have a pleasant surprise. 當他回來時,他會有個愉快的驚喜。

▶ As soon as you **finish**, please tell me. 你一做完,就請告訴我。

(e) 與「旅行」有關的來去動詞(如 come、go、leave、arrive 等)常用現在簡單式表示「已經計劃好的未來動作」。

USAGE PRACTICE

▶ The train **leaves** the station at a quarter to one. 這班火車在十二點四十五分離站。

▶ The plane **arrives** at Narita Airport at 10 a.m. 這班飛機在上午十點抵達成田機場。

▶ We **arrive** at the airport in a few minutes' time. 幾分鐘後我們會到達機場。

▶ The mail **arrives** at this town in the evening. 郵件在傍晚到達這城鎮。

▶ He **departs** for London on Thursday morning. 他星期四早上離開前往倫敦。

▶ He **departs** on Monday morning and **arrives** here on Tuesday night.
他會在星期一早上出發,並在星期二晚上到達這裡。

▶ We **get off** at Long Pier and **take** a ferry across to Clearwater Island.
我們在長碼頭下船,然後再搭渡船去清水島。

▶ They **leave** for Sonia Town on Saturday. 他們會在星期六前往索尼亞城。

(f) 現在簡單式也常用於比賽的實況報導或戲劇劇本。為了要讓比賽更加生動、有趣,播報員常常使用現在簡單式。

USAGE PRACTICE

▶ "Tony **dashes** out with the ball. It **is snatched** away by Pepe. Pepe **runs** all the way down the field. He **passes** the ball to Max..."

「東尼帶球衝出去，球被培培奪走，培培一路跑過球場，他把球傳給馬克斯…」

▶ "Jill **snatches** the ball from Brenda and **throws** it to Nancy. Nancy **tries** to evade the defenders..." 「吉兒從布蘭達那邊奪走球，然後傳給南茜。南茜試著要閃過防守的人…」

▶ "He **takes** the shuttlecock and **sends** it high above the net."

「他拿起羽毛球，高高地把它打過網。」

▶ "A witch **waves** her wand over the child and **says**, 'Behold! A needle will prick her finger and she will die!' Then, with a loud laugh, the witch **flies** away."

「巫婆在孩子的頭上揮舞著魔杖，說：『看！有一根針將會刺到她的手指，然後她將死亡！』接著，大笑一聲，巫婆就飛走了」。

▶ "Lady Jane **hurries** but her heel **gets** caught in the carpet on the stairs and she **falls** headlong..." 「珍女士急忙趕去，但是她的鞋跟卡到樓梯的地毯，她頭朝前地跌倒…」

▶ "James Bond **drives** his car to Monte Carlo. On the way, he **stops** and **gives** a lift to..."

「詹姆士‧龐德開車去蒙地卡羅。在路上，他停下車順便搭載…」

(g) 現在簡單式也可以用在感歎句、宣布或實地示範的時候，表示「在目前實際正發生的事情」。

USAGE PRACTICE

▶ Here **comes** the train! 火車來了！

▶ There he **goes!** 他走了！

▶ The cook **measures** a hundred grams of flour and **mixes** it with some sugar. He **beats** in some **eggs** until... 廚師量了一百公克的麵粉，並將它與一些糖混合。他打蛋直到…

小練習

請根據提示在空格中填入正確的現在式動詞。

1. He _____ (*change*) his uniform every day.

2. She usually _____ (*wake*) up early.

3. It _____ (*not rain*) much in winter.

4. We always _____ (*play*) football; we _____ (*not play*) hockey.

5. "_____ you _____ (*smoke*) a pipe?" "No, I _____ (*do not*)."

6. He _____ (*take*) part in the fire-walking ceremony every year.

7. He sometimes _____ (*put*) his money in the bank.

8. As soon as the shop _____ (*open*), go to buy some batteries for the radio.

9. When she _____ (*meet*) elderly people, she _____ (*be*) usually shy.

10. The warehouses _____ (*provide*) storage space for goods brought in by the boats which _____ (*serve*) the port.

11. The earth _____ (*be*) round. It _____ (*revolve*) around the sun and _____ (*rotate*) on its own axis.

12. She _____ (*clean*) her room once a month. She _____ (*not clean*) it every week.

13. I _____ (*live*) near the post office. I _____ (*walk*) there every morning to mail my letters. I _____ (*not mind*) when my friends _____ (*ask*) me to buy stamps or mail their letters for them.

☞ 更多相關習題請見本章應用練習 Part 1～Part 4。

10-2 過去簡單式

(a) 過去簡單式的否定句和疑問句必須使用助動詞 did。

USAGE PRACTICE		
肯定句	否定句	疑問句
▶ She **went** home.	→ She **did not go** home.	→ **Did** she **go** home?
她回家去了。	她沒有回家去。	她回家去了嗎？
▶ She **broke** it.	→ She **did not break** it.	→ **Did** she **break** it?
她打破它了。	她沒有打破它。	她打破它了嗎？
▶ They **scolded** him.	→ They **did not scold** him.	→ **Did** they **scold** him?
他們責罵他。	他們沒有責罵他。	他們責罵他了嗎？
▶ I **ate** it.	→ I **did not eat** it.	→ **Did** I **eat** it?
我吃了它。	我沒有吃它。	我吃了它嗎？

(b) 過去簡單式表示「在過去某一明確時間發生或完成的動作」，常與表示過去的時間

副詞連用。

USAGE PRACTICE

▶ They **made** these chairs all by themselves. 這些椅子全都是他們自己做的。

▶ They **bought** the things when they **went** to Japan. 他們去日本時,買了這些東西。

▶ He **left** the house an hour ago. 他在一小時以前離開這房子了。

▶ **Did** he tell you when he **arrived**? 他有告訴你他何時到達嗎?

▶ She **spoke** to me just now. 她剛才和我說過話。

▶ She **studied** French when she **was** in school. 當她在學校時,她學過法文。

▶ She **went** to the hospital yesterday. 她昨天去了醫院。

▶ She **had** a medical check up last week. 上星期她做了身體檢查。

▶ We **stopped** for a drink on the way. 我們在中途停下來喝一杯。

▶ We **visited** Uncle Peter in December. 我們在十二月時拜訪了彼得叔叔。

▶ The goods **arrived** early this morning. 貨物在今天清晨到達。

▶ **Did** you **help** him up when he **fell** down the stairs?

他摔下樓梯時,你有幫忙讓他站起來嗎?

▶ A thief **stole** her purse last night. 昨晚一個小偷偷了她的錢包。

 過去簡單式可以表示「一連串的過去動作」。

▶ The sun **shone** when we **went** out. 當我們出門時,太陽照耀著。

▶ I **saw** her when she **passed** my house. 當她經過我家時,我看見她。

▶ She **came** home around noon, **bathed**, **ate** lunch and **went** out again.

她在中午左右回家、洗過澡、吃了午餐,接著又出門了。

▶ First, he **worked** in a store. Then, he **found** a job in a bank but **left** it to work in an insurance company. He **liked** the job and **kept** it for the rest of his life.

最初,他在一家商店工作。然後,他找到在銀行的工作,但是又離職去一家保險公司任職。他喜歡這份工作,而且終其一生從事這一行。

▶ He **got** out of bed, **stretched** himself, **walked** to the window, and **opened** it.

他起床、伸展一下、走向窗戶,並且打開它。

(c) 過去簡單式可以表示「過去的習慣」,常與 always、often 或 never 等頻率副詞連用。

▶ We always **visited** her whenever we **had** the time. 我們一有時間總會去探望她。

▶ She always **did** as she **was told**. 她總是照別人告訴她的話去做。

▶ They always **brought** us candy when they **visited** us.

他們來拜訪我們時，總會帶糖果給我們。

▶ He always **played** for high stakes. 他總是下大賭注。

▶ When I **was** younger, I often **went** fishing in that river.

當我年輕的時候，我常在那條河釣魚。

▶ I often **accompanied** my father on his inspection tours. 我常常陪我爸爸去做巡迴檢查。

▶ I **stayed** with them quite often when I **was** small. 當我小時候，常和他們一起住。

▶ He never **played** with us. 他從來不和我們一起玩。

▶ Her mother never **allowed** her to play out of doors. 她的媽媽從不允許她去戶外玩。

▶ She never **said** a word against him. 她從未說過反對他的話。

(d) 在過去式中，當直接引句轉為間接引句時，要用過去簡單式代替現在簡單式。

▶ "I think it is the best way," he replied. 「我認為這是最好的方法。」他回答說。（直接引句）

　　→ He replied that he **thought** it **was** the best way.

　　　他回答說他認為這是最好的方法。（間接引句）

▶ She asked, "Where is Peter?" 她問：「彼得在哪裡？」（直接引句）

　　→ She asked where Peter **was**. 她問彼得在哪裡。（間接引句）

▶ "I love fishing," he said. 他說：「我愛釣魚。」（直接引句）

　　→ He said that he **loved** fishing. 他說他愛釣魚。（間接引句）

▶ "I always swim in that lake," she said. 「我總是在那個湖裡游泳。」她說。（直接引句）

　　→ She said that she always **swam** in that lake. 她說她總在那個湖裡游泳。（間接引句）

▶ "I know what it means," he said. 「我知道這是什麼意思。」他說。（直接引句）

　　→ He said that he **knew** what it **meant**. 他說他知道這是什麼意思。（間接引句）

(e) 在假設語氣中，過去簡單式用來表示「與現在事實相反」。

▶ If I **had** a lot of money, I **would tour** the world. 如果我有很多錢，我就會環遊世界。

▶ If you **asked** him nicely, he **would tell** you the answer.

如果你好好地問他，他會告訴你答案。

▶ She **would pass** the examination if she **worked** hard. 如果她努力讀書，她會通過考試。

▶ I wish I **lived** there. 但願我住在那裡。

 有關假設語氣的詳細說明請見 **12-2**。

請根據提示在空格中填入正確的過去式動詞。

1. He _____ (*be*) very pleased at my success.

2. She _____ (*wake*) up early in the morning and _____ (*prepare*) breakfast for us.

3. It _____ (*be*) two nights ago that he _____ (*have*) that nightmare.

4. Have you finished reading the book I _____ (*lend*) you last week?

5. I _____ (*use*) up most of my money when I _____ (*be*) in Maple Town.

6. She _____ (*wear*) a bright-red dress.

7. I _____ (*boil*) the water and _____ (*make*) some tea for the visitors.

8. I _____ (*not break*) any of these glasses. Someone else _____ (*break*) them.

9. She is sure she _____ (*not have*) the keys with her when she _____ (*leave*) the house.

10. I know definitely that it _____ (*be*) Terry whom I _____ (see) walking down the street this morning.

11. They _____ (*think*) that it _____ (*be*) not a very good plan, and they _____ (*tell*) us so.

12. He _____ (*shout*) that they _____ (*need*) help at once.

13. I _____ (*take*) the book from him, _____ (*glance*) through it quickly, and then _____ (*give*) it back to him.

14. He _____ (*reply*) that he _____ (*be*) through with this business and that he _____ (*plan*) to go abroad for a short holiday.

15. I was walking along the road when I _____ (*see*) an accident. A car _____ (*skid*) off

the road, _____ (*bump*) into a cyclist, and _____ (*smash*) into a lamp post.

☞ 更多相關習題請見本章應用練習 Part 5～Part 6。

10-3 未來簡單式

(a) 未來簡單式是用來表示「未來的動作」，動詞要改成「will + 原形動詞」。will 的否定型態 will not 可以縮寫為 won't。

USAGE PRACTICE		
肯定句	否定句	疑問句
▶ I **will be** there.	→ I **won't be** there.	→ **Will** I **be** there?
我將會在那裡。	我將不會在那裡。	我將會在那裡嗎？
▶ I **will tell** him.	→ I **will not tell** him.	→ **Will** I **tell** him?
我會告訴他。	我不會告訴他。	我將會告訴他嗎？
▶ He **will find** it.	→ He **won't find** it.	→ **Will** he **find** it?
他將會找到它。	他將找不到它。	他將會找到它嗎？
▶ She **will send** it.	→ She **will not send** it.	→ **Will** she send it?
她將會寄它。	她將不會寄它。	她將會寄它嗎？
▶ You **will know**.	→ You **won't know**.	→ **Will** you **know**?
你將會知道。	你將不會知道。	你將會知道嗎？
▶ They **will eat** it.	→ They **won't eat** it.	→ **Will** they **eat** it?
他們將會吃它。	他們將不會吃它。	他們將會吃它嗎？
▶ It **will bite** you.	→ It **won't bite** you.	→ **Will** it **bite** you?
牠將會咬你。	牠將不會咬你。	牠將會咬你嗎？

 注意 主詞是第一人稱（I 或 we）時，原本應該要用「shall + 原形動詞」，但現在這種說法僅用在正式文字、提議或附加問句中。

▶ I **shall not** let it happen. 我將不會讓它發生。

▶ **Shall** we wait? 我們該等嗎？

▶ Let's talk, **shall** we? 我們來談談吧，好嗎？

(b) 未來簡單式也可以表示「沒有計畫或不確定的未來動作」。

USAGE PRACTICE

▶ I **won't understand** what he means if he talks in French.

如果他説法文，我就會不懂他的意思了。

▶ Where **will** I **be** after five years, I wonder?　我想知道五年後我會在哪裡？

▶ We **will stay** with our aunt for the holidays.　假日時，我們將與阿姨一起住。

▶ **Will** we **give** away these old magazines?　我們要把這些舊雜誌丟掉嗎？

▶ **Will** they **arrive** in time for the meeting?　他們將會及時來開會嗎？

▶ **Will** she **cry** if you scold her?　如果你責罵她，她會哭嗎？

▶ She **will obey** whatever orders she is given.　她會服從任何給她的命令。

▶ He **will give** it to you if you ask him.　如果你要求他，他會把它送給你。

▶ They **will not listen** to anything I say.　他們將不會聽從我説的任何話。

▶ Perhaps Janet **will come**.　也許珍妮會來。

▶ I don't think that there **will be** any tickets left.　我不認為會有任何票剩下來。

▶ The leaves **will fall** when autumn comes.　當秋天來時，葉子會掉下來。

▶ For how long **will** the earth **exist**?　地球還會存在多久？

▶ The plants **will die** if it doesn't rain soon.　如果不快點下雨，植物會死。

 但是，對於說話當時已經計劃好的未來動作，也可使用未來簡單式。

▶ "Oh, there's no butter left! I **will get** some in the morning."

「噢，沒有牛油了！我早上要去買一些。」

▶ I **will return** in half an hour.　我將在半小時內回來。

▶ I **will do** my work tomorrow. I **will help** you this afternoon.

我明天將會做我的工作，今天下午我會幫你。

(c) 未來簡單式也可以表示「聲明」或「命令」。

USAGE PRACTICE

▶ You **will do** as I tell you; do you hear me?　你要照我説的話去做，聽到沒有？

▶ Classes **will start** at half past seven.　七點半開始上課。

▶ School **will reopen** next week.　學校將在下週復課。

▶ The flight for Paris **will take off** in an hour.　往巴黎的班機將在一小時後起飛。

▶ Passengers **will board** the airplane now. 乘客現在即將登機。

▶ Now, here are your duties for tomorrow: Tony **will clean** the blackboard, and Mark **will arrange** the desks. 好，這是你們明天的職務：東尼要擦黑板，而馬克要排桌子。

▶ I **will give** you the orders now. You **will not interrupt** me until I have finished. Then, you **will carry out** your duties accordingly.

現在我會給你命令。我還沒有説完之前你不能插話。然後，你得照著執行職務。

(d) be going to 是另一種表達未來式的用法。

USAGE PRACTICE		
肯定句	否定句	疑問句
▶ I **am going to** watch TV.	→ I **am not going to** watch TV.	→ **Am** I **going to** watch TV?
我要去看電視。	我不要去看電視。	我要去看電視嗎？
▶ He **is going to** see it.	→ He **isn't going to** see it.	→ **Is** he **going to** see it?
他要去看它。	他不要去看它。	他要去看它嗎？

(e) be going to 表示「已經計劃好要做的動作」，句中不一定要有表示「時間」的副詞或副詞片語；如果沒有，就表示「不久的將來確定會發生的事」。

USAGE PRACTICE
▶ I **am going to** write a letter to him tonight. 我將在今晚寫一封信給他。
▶ We **are going to** the movies tonight. 今晚我們要去看電影。
▶ He **is going to** wash his scooter this evening. 他今晚要洗他的摩托車。
▶ I **am not going to** see him this evening. 今晚我不會去看他。
▶ He **is going to** give it to you since you like it so much.
既然你這麼喜歡它，他會把它送給你。
▶ They **are going to** make the birthday cake tomorrow. 明天他們要做生日蛋糕。
▶ They **aren't going to** climb that mountain tomorrow. 他們明天將不會去爬那座山。
▶ I'**m going to** borrow his bicycle. 我將要借他的腳踏車。
▶ He saved up some money. He **is going to** buy a car. 他已經存了一些錢。他將會買車。
▶ She **is going to** be a nurse when she grows up. 當她長大時，她將會當護士。

▶ She **is not going** to accept your payment for the book. 她不會收你這本書的錢。

▶ We **are going to** watch television. 我們將要看電視。

▶ **Are** we **going to** tell him when he asks us? 他問我們的時候，我們要告訴他嗎？

▶ They **aren't going to** tell us the answer. It's no use asking them.

　他們不會告訴我們答案，問他們也沒用的。

▶ When **are** you **going to** return my book? 你什麼時候會歸還我的書呢？

▶ Look out! That tree **is going to** fall! 小心！那棵樹要倒了！

▶ Help! I**'m going to** drown! 救命啊！我要淹死了！

▶ The cow looks very ill. I think it**'s going to** die.

　這頭母牛看起來病得很重，我想牠快要死了。

▶ Turn off the switch. The soup **is going to** boil over. 把開關關掉，湯要沸騰溢出了。

▶ Look at the clouds. It **is going to** rain. 看看這些雲，快要下雨了。

▶ The wind **is going to** blow the fence down. 這風快要把籬笆吹倒了。

 請比較下列未來簡單式的涵義。

▶ The sky is overcast. It **is going to** rain. 天空烏雲密佈，快下雨了。（可能性大）

▶ It's been such a hot day. I hope it **will** rain soon. 天氣一直很熱，我希望快下雨。（可能性小）

▶ He **is going to** stop at the library. 他將會在圖書館逗留。（確定）

▶ He **will** stop at the library, **won't** he? 他會在圖書館逗留，不是嗎？（不確定）

(f) 表示「依照意志執行而非外在因素（如時間、條件等）的動作」，多用 be going to；
　 而 will 常用於「被外在因素、而非個人因素所影響的未來事件」。

USAGE PRACTICE

▶ He **is going to** sell his house. 他將要賣房子。（因為他自己想賣）

▶ He **will** sell his house. 他將會賣房子。（因為負債或其他外在因素）

▶ He **is going to** give it to you. 他將會把它給你。（因為他自己願意）

▶ He **will** give it to you if you ask him. 如果你要求，他會把它給你。（因為你要求）

▶ He **is going to** study hard. 他會努力讀書。（因為他自己想這麼做）

▶ He **will study** hard. 他將會努力讀書。（因為他必須準備考試）

(g) 未來簡單式常與無進行式形的動詞連用，以表示未來的動作。

▶ She **will believe** whatever you say. 無論你説什麼她都會相信。

▶ She **will see** through your disguise immediately. 她會馬上看穿你的偽裝。

▶ I **will hear** your side of the story first. 我會先聽你們這方的説法。

▶ It **will matter** a lot to her. 這對她會很重要。

▶ I **will look like** a fool if I do that. 如果我那樣做，我會看起來像傻子。

▶ No one **will believe** your story. 沒有人會相信你的故事。

▶ They **will notice** that something is wrong. 他們會注意到有問題。

▶ I **will feel** out of place at the party. 在宴會中，我會覺得格格不入。

▶ I hope she **will remember** to bring it. 我希望她會記得帶它。

小練習

請根據提示在空格中填入正確的未來式動詞（限用 will）。

1. The servant _____ (*polish*) the silver in the morning.

2. I _____ (*refuse*) his offer to deliver the goods next week.

3. You _____ (*not disappoint*) us, _____ you?

4. She _____ (*be*) fifty years old on Wednesday.

5. They _____ (*celebrate*) their wedding anniversary next month.

6. _____ you _____ (*go*) with me to that shop tomorrow? It _____ (*be*) open by eight.

7. He _____ (*not clear*) away the rubbish from the road unless he is paid to do so.

8. The food in the refrigerator _____ (*last*) us for a week.

9. We _____ (*play*) tennis this afternoon if it does not rain.

10. _____ you _____ (*buy*) tickets for the show tonight?

11. Your parents _____ (*not be*) pleased if you stay out until three o'clock the next morning.

12. When _____ we _____ (*meet*) you again?

13. _____ you _____ (*not listen*) to our advice and put the machine in the garage?

☞ 更多相關習題請見本章應用練習 Part 7～Part 11。

10-4 現在進行式

(a) 現在進行式主要是由「am/are/is + 現在分詞」構成。

USAGE PRACTICE		
肯定句	否定句	疑問句
▶ I **am writing**. 我正在寫作。	→ I **am not writing**. 我沒有正在寫作。	→ **Am** I **writing**? 我正在寫作嗎？
▶ She **is laughing**. 她正在笑。	→ She **is not laughing**. 她沒有在笑。	→ **Is** she **laughing**? 她正在笑嗎？
▶ She **is coming** here for the holidays. 她將會來這裡渡假。	→ She **is not coming** here for the holidays. 她將不會來這裡渡假。	→ **Is** she **coming** here for the holidays? 她將會來這渡假嗎？
▶ We **are reading**. 我們正在閱讀。	→ We **are not reading**. 我們沒有正在閱讀。	→ **Are** we **reading**? 我們正在閱讀嗎？
▶ They **are running**. 他們正在跑步。	→ They **are not running**. 他們沒有正在跑步。	→ **Are** they **running**? 他們正在跑步嗎？
▶ They **are leaving** now. 他們現在正要離開。	→ They **are not leaving** now. 他們現在沒有正要離開。	→ **Are** they **leaving** now? 他們現在正要離開嗎？
▶ **It** is raining. 正在下雨。	→ It **is not raining**. 沒有在下雨。	→ **Is** it **raining**? 正在下雨嗎？

(b) 現在進行式表示「現在正在發生的動作」。

USAGE PRACTICE
▶ I **am telling** you the truth. 我正在告訴你事實。
▶ Why **are** you **crying**? 為什麼你在哭？
▶ She **is waiting** for the bus now. 她現在正在等公車。
▶ She **is not studying** now. 她現在沒有在讀書。
▶ My mother **is cooking** now. 我媽媽現在正在做飯。

▶ He **is climbing** the ladder. 他正在爬梯子。

▶ Alex **is coming** out of his house now. 艾力克斯現在正從他家走出來。

▶ **Is** the tailor **sewing** your dress now? 裁縫師現在正在縫製你的洋裝嗎？

▶ They **are drinking** coffee. 他們正在喝咖啡。

▶ The children **are not playing** in the field now. 孩子們現在沒有在運動場上玩耍。

▶ **Is** the water **boiling**? 水正在沸騰嗎？

▶ **Is** the sun **shining**? 太陽正照耀著嗎？

(c) 主動詞如果是來去動詞（如 go、come、arrive、move 等），則現在進行式也可以
表示「即將發生的動作」，並常與表示「未來」的時間副詞或片語連用。

USAGE PRACTICE

▶ I **am going** to town this afternoon. 今天下午我要到鎮上去。

▶ I **am going** to the movies tonight. 今晚我要去看電影。

▶ I **am not going** anywhere tomorrow. 明天我什麼地方都不去。

▶ **Are** you **coming** with me? 你要和我一起來嗎？

▶ **Are** you **going** anywhere for the weekend? 你這個週末要去哪裡？

▶ **Aren't** you **going** to the party tomorrow night? 你們不參加明天晚上的宴會嗎？

▶ Thomas **is coming** here next week. 湯瑪斯下週要來這裡。

▶ He **isn't coming** to the meeting tomorrow. 他明天不會來開會。

▶ My cousin **is going** to Nada next month. 我的表弟下個月要去娜達。

▶ The man next door **is moving** out at the end of the month.

住在隔壁的男子這個月底要搬走。

▶ My brother **is leaving** for Hawaii on Tuesday. 我的哥哥星期二要前往夏威夷。

▶ She **is going** home next week. 她下週將要回家。

▶ She **is coming** here to spend the day with us. 她將要來這裡和我們共渡一天。

▶ **Are** we **moving** into the new house next week? 我們下個星期要搬進新家嗎？

▶ We **are going** to see him next Monday. 我們下星期一要去看他。

▶ We **are taking** a bus to Cherry Park in the afternoon. 我們下午要搭公車去櫻桃公園。

▶ When **are** we **going** home? 我們要什麼時候回家呢？

▶ They **are going** to the airport this evening. 他們今晚要去機場。

► They **are flying** to Canada next week. 下週他們將要搭飛機去加拿大。

► They **are going** back to school next Monday. 他們下週一將要返校。

► **Are** they **coming** this afternoon? 他們今天下午會來嗎？

► They **are coming** home by ship. 他們將要搭船回家。

(d) 現在進行式也可以表示「即將進行已經計劃好的未來動作」，也常與表示「未來」的時間副詞或片語連用。

USAGE PRACTICE

► **Are** you **doing** anything this evening? 你今晚有事要做嗎？

► **Are** you **joining** us at the picnic on Saturday? 你們要參加我們星期六的野餐嗎？

► She **isn't singing** in the choir tomorrow. 她明天不去合唱團唱歌。

► My sister **is getting** married this October. 我姊姊十月要結婚。

► They **are taking part** in the race tomorrow. 他們明天要參加賽跑。

► We **are visiting** Aunt Sally on Saturday. 星期六我們要去拜訪莎莉阿姨。

► **Are** they **visiting** the museum on Monday? 他們將在星期一參觀博物館嗎？

(e) 現在進行式可以表示 「經常重覆的習慣性動作」，常與頻率副詞 always 或 continually 連用，有時含有「責備」的意味；此用法比較常在口語會話中出現，在書面文字上則比較少見。

USAGE PRACTICE

► She **is** always **asking** silly questions. 她總是問一些蠢問題。

► She **is** always **losing** her temper with the children. 她老是對孩子們發脾氣。

► She **is** continually **losing** her glasses. 她老是弄丟她的眼鏡。

► He **is** always **banging** the door shut. 他總是砰地一聲把門關上。

► He **is** always **eating** ice cream. 他老是在吃冰淇淋。

► They **are** always **arguing** with each other. 他們總是彼此爭吵不休。

► They **are** always **doing** that sort of thing. 他們總是做那種事。

► The dog **is** always **chasing** the cat. 這隻狗總是追著那隻貓。

(f) 有些動詞不能用進行式，即使是用來表示正在發生的動作或持續存在的情形，也只

能用現在簡單式來表達。

USAGE PRACTICE

表示「心智狀況」的動詞，如 think、know、recognize、understand、believe、desire、wish、like、hate、want、love、realize、forget、remember 等。

▶ I **remember** him quite clearly.　我很清楚記得他這個人。

▶ I **remember** she wore that dress last time.　我記得她上次穿那件洋裝。

▶ They **wish** to go home now.　他們希望現在回家去。

▶ I **wish** I were an adult.　但願我是個成年人。

▶ She **thinks** everybody likes her.　她認為人人都喜歡她。

▶ I **think** that you should go now.　我認為你現在應該走了。

▶ She **loves** the color.　她愛這個顏色。

▶ I simply **dislike** getting wet.　我就是不喜歡弄溼。

▶ He **hates** to be treated like that.　他討厭被那樣對待。

▶ I **hate** a person who would do such a cruel thing.　我討厭一個會做這麼殘忍的事的人。

▶ We **want** to go home now.　我們現在想回家了。

▶ I **want** to have my bath now.　我現在想洗個澡。

▶ We **know** them very well.　我們跟他們很熟。

▶ She **knows** the truth.　她知道真相。

▶ We **understand** the situation very well.　我們非常了解這情況。

感官動詞，如 feel、see、hear、taste、smell 等。

▶ I **feel** very hot. Can you please switch on the fan?　我覺得很熱。可以請你開電扇嗎？

▶ I **see** a girl playing with a kitten.　我看到一個女孩在和小貓玩耍。

▶ "Do you smell anything?" "Yes, I **smell** something burning."

　「你有聞到什麼味道嗎？」「有，我聞到某個東西燒焦的味道」。

▶ I **hear** someone walking up the stairs.　我聽到有人上樓。

▶ I **hear** the roar of thunder.　我聽到轟隆隆的雷聲。

▶ She **hears** someone calling.　她聽到有人打電話來。

一般動詞 have 表示「擁有，患（病）」之意時。

▶ I **have** the key to the safe.　我有保險箱的鑰匙。

▶ We **have** the brightest classroom in the school. 我們有全校最明亮的教室。

▶ Betty **has** a cold. She is sneezing all the time. 蓓蒂感冒了，她一直在打噴嚏。

▶ We **have** a lot of homework to do today. 我們今天有許多家庭作業要做。

其他動詞或片語，如 seem、appear、possess、own、contain、consist of、matter、suppose、belong、owe、mind、keep on、cost 等。

▶ It **seems** that he dislikes that girl. 他似乎不喜歡那個女孩子。

▶ She **seems** a nice girl. 她似乎是個好女孩。

▶ Fruits **contain** a good deal of vitamins. 水果含有大量的維生素。

▶ The jar **contains** peanut butter. 罐子裡裝了花生醬。

▶ I **suppose** that is the only way to do it. 我猜想那是唯一的做法。

▶ Do you **suppose** that it might happen again? 你猜這件事可能會再發生嗎？

▶ She **owes** me an apology. 她欠我一個道歉。

▶ Do you **mind** if I leave now? 你介意我現在離開嗎？

▶ He **keeps on** asking me for more money. 他一直向我要更多的錢。

▶ The team **consists of** eleven players. 這個球隊由十一個球員組成。

 以上某些動詞只有在表示特殊意義或有目的的動作時，才能使用現在進行式。例如，一般動詞 have 表示「做…」、「吃…」時，就可以用進行式。

▶ My brother **is having** his bath. 我弟弟正在洗澡。

▶ We **are having** dinner at the restaurant tonight. 今晚我們將在餐廳吃晚餐。

▶ I **am seeing** my brother off at the station. 我要在車站為我哥哥送行。

▶ She **is thinking** about her next assignment. 她正在思索下一份作業。

▶ The judge **is hearing** a case at the court tomorrow. 明天法官要在法庭聽審。

請根據提示在空格中填入正確的現在進行式動詞。

1. The clerks _____ (*sort*) out the letters.

2. She _____ (*paint*) some posters for her room.

3. I _____ (*help*) her this evening. _____ you _____ (*come*) along, too?

4. The men _____ (*unload*) the crates of fruit from the truck.

5. She _____ (*wash*) her clothes. She _____ (*not iron*) them.

6. We _____ (*pack*) our luggage now. We _____ (*leave*) for Newtown on Monday.

7. Tonight they _____ (*sleep*) in the guest room.

8. _____ the boys _____ (*whistle*) in the next room? Tell them that I _____ (*work*) now and that I don't like to be disturbed.

9. The doctor _____ (*make*) a speech afterward. You should all be silent while he _____ (*speak*).

10. The ship _____ (*leave*) for Port Haven in two days. Many people _____ (*travel*) on it.

11. We _____ (*learn*) how to use the washing machine. We _____ (*put*) our clothes into it now. Mother _____ (*turn*) on the switch.

12. There has just been a robbery at the jeweler's shop. A police car _____ (*come*) along the road. It _____ (*stop*) in front of the shop. Many people _____ (*gather*) around the shop.

13. He _____ (*tell*) a lie. He _____ (*not repair*) your radio this evening. He _____ (*go*) to the movies with his friends.

14. _____ you _____ (*pay*) attention to the lesson? I _____ (*give*) you a test on it tomorrow.

☞ 更多相關習題請見本章應用練習 Part 12～Part 19。

10-5 過去進行式

(a) 過去進行式主要是由「was/were + 過去分詞」構成。

USAGE PRACTICE		
肯定句	否定句	疑問句
▶ She **was reading** a book. 她當時正在讀書。	→ She **was not reading** a book. 她當時沒有在讀書。	→ **Was** she **reading** a book? 她當時正在讀書嗎？
▶ They **were cleaning** the shelves. 他們當時正在清理架子。	→ They **weren't cleaning** the shelves. 他們當時沒有在清理架子。	→ **Were** they **cleaning** the shelves? 他們當時正在清理架子嗎？

(b) 過去進行式表示「在過去某個時候正在進行的動作」，常與表示過去的時間副詞或片語連用。

▶ She **was sewing** a new dress all yesterday afternoon.　她昨天一整個下午都在縫製新洋裝。

▶ He **was having** his dinner at seven o'clock.　七點鐘的時候他正在吃晚飯。

▶ I **was waiting** for him then.　我那時正在等他。

▶ At four o'clock we **were having** tea.　四點時，我們正在喝茶。

(c) 過去進行式可以用來表示「在過去某個時候正在進行的兩個動作」，常與連接詞 while 或 as 連用。

▶ I **was sweeping** the floor while my sister **was sewing**.　當我姊姊在縫衣服時，我正在掃地。

▶ He **was studying** while I **was watching** television.　當我正在看電視的時候，他正在讀書。

▶ While he was **chatting** with her, we **were buying** the groceries.
當他在和她聊天時，我們正在買雜貨。

▶ The boys **were singing** while the girls **were dancing**.
當女孩們在跳舞的時候，男孩們正在唱歌。

▶ She **was humming** a tune while she **was cooking**.　她一邊煮飯，一邊哼著曲子。

▶ She **was crying** with pain as he **was bandaging** her arm.
當他正在用繃帶包紮她的手臂時，她痛得大叫。

▶ They **were watching** as the players **were practicing**.　當球員在練習時，他們正在觀看。

(d) 過去進行式和簡單過去式可以在同一個句子中使用，表示「過去某個動作在另一動作發生時正在進行中」。此種用法常與連接詞 when、while 或 as 連用。

▶ When I reached the place, it **was** already **getting** dark.
當我到達那地方時，天色已漸漸變暗了。

▶ When I **was having** a shower, I slipped and fell.　當我正在洗澡的時候，我滑了一跤跌倒。

▶ The guests arrived while I **was** still **cooking**.　當我還在煮飯時，客人到達了。

▶ As he **was cycling** to school, he saw an accident. 當他正騎著單車上學時，他看見一場意外。

▶ He **was driving** when the accident **happened**. 意外發生時，他正在開車。

▶ I saw her when she **was passing** my house. 當她正經過我家時，我看見她。

▶ The sun **was shining** when we went out. 當我們出門時，太陽正閃耀。

▶ They **were talking** about her when she came into the room.

當她進來房間時，他們正在談論她。

▶ A thief entered the house while they **were sleeping**. 小偷在他們在睡覺的時候進入屋子。

(e) 過去進行式可以表示「過去的習慣」，常與 always、often、constantly 等副詞連用。

USAGE PRACTICE

▶ They **were** always **swimming** in the sea. 他們過去常在海裡游泳。

▶ She **was** always **buying** new dresses in London. 過去她總是在倫敦買新衣。

▶ She **was** always **talking** about herself. 過去她總是談論關於自己的事。

▶ Sally **was** often **making** the same mistake. 過去莎莉常常犯同樣的錯誤。

▶ He **was** often **driving** his father's car. 他以前經常開他父親的車。

▶ He **was** constantly **grumbling** to himself. 過去他經常自言自語發牢騷。

▶ The old man **was** constantly **muttering** to himself. 過去這老人經常喃喃自語。

(f) 當直接引句改成間接引句時，如果時間點是在過去，就要使用過去進行式代替現在進行式。

USAGE PRACTICE

▶ "I am going home," he said. 「我要回家了。」他說。（直接引句）

　→ He said that he **was going** home. 他說他要回家了。（間接引句）

▶ "Where are they playing?" she asked me. 「他們在哪裡玩？」，她問我。（直接引句）

　→ She asked me where they **were playing**. 她問我他們在哪裡玩。（間接引句）

▶ "I am studying," he said. 「我正在讀書。」他說。（直接引句）

　→ He said that he **was studying**. 他說他正在讀書。（間接引句）

請根據提示在空格中填入正確的過去進行式動詞。

1. What _____ she _____ (*do*) when you went to her house?

2. She _____ (*bake*) some cakes for her sister's birthday.

3. He _____ (*do*) some experiments on frogs when I visited him.

4. None of them _____ (*dance*) although the band _____ (*play*) a waltz.

5. While I _____ (*stroll*) by the river, I saw a policeman chasing a thief.

6. I could not see anything because of the people who _____ (*stand*) in front of me.

7. I found a ten dollar bill while I _____ (*search*) for my pen.

8. Two men _____ (*follow*) him when he came here.

9. She _____ (*eat*) lunch, and the baby _____ (*play*) in the room when I went to see her.

10. When I last saw her, she _____ (*get*) into a car. All I noticed was that she _____ (*wear*) black shoes.

11. I _____ (*listen*) to the radio while my sister _____ (*watch*) television.

12. As I _____ (*shop*) near the post office, I saw Anna. She _____ (*sit*) in a café with her cousin.

13. They _____ certainly not _____ (*talk*) about you. They _____ (*discuss*) the arrival of the new manager.

14. "What _____ she _____ (*do*) the whole of yesterday morning?" "Oh, she _____ (*look*) after her nieces, and she _____ (*make*) some jam tarts at the same time."

☞ 更多相關習題請見本章應用練習 Part 20～Part 26。

10-6 未來進行式

(a) 未來進行式主要是由「will + be + 現在分詞」構成。

USAGE PRACTICE		
肯定句	否定句	疑問句
▶ I will be going.	→ I will not be going.	→ Will I be going?
我將要去。	我將不會去。	我將要去嗎？

She **will be eating**.	→ She **will not be eating**.	→ **Will** she **be eating**?
她將會在吃。	她將不會在吃。	她將會在吃嗎？
He **will be waiting**.	→ He **will not be waiting**.	→ **Will** he **be waiting**?
他將會在等。	他將不會在等。	他將會在等嗎？
They **will be working**.	→ They **won't be working**.	→ **Will** they **be working**?
他們將在工作。	他們將不會在工作。	他們將會在工作嗎？

(b) 未來進行式可以表示「在未來某一時間將會進行某一沒有計畫的動作」，可與表示未來的時間副詞或片語連用。

USAGE PRACTICE

▶ You'd better hurry home now; your mother **will be worrying** about you.

你最好現在快點回家；你媽媽會擔心你。

▶ She **will be needing** the instruments again. 她將會再需要這些儀器。

▶ They **will be rehearsing** for the play soon. 他們將很快為這齣戲排演。

▶ They **will be seeing** you again, won't they? 他們將會與你再見面，不是嗎？

▶ We **will be writing** an essay on the same topic. 我們將要寫一篇題目相同的短文。

▶ **Will** it **be snowing** when they arrive in London?

當他們抵達倫敦的時候，那裡會正在下雪嗎？

▶ The bus **will be coming** up again to fetch us. 這公車將會再來接我們。

(c) 未來進行式可以表示「在未來某一時間將會進行的例行或預定的動作」，可與表示未來的時間副詞或片語連用。

USAGE PRACTICE

▶ I **will be doing** my homework all evening. 我整個晚上都將會在做功課。

▶ This time next month, I **will be enjoying** myself in Japan.

下個月的這個時候，我將正在日本玩得很愉快。

▶ Don't come at seven o'clock. I **will be sleeping** then. 別在七點來，那時我將會在睡覺。

▶ I **will be seeing** Alice in school tomorrow. I can give her the message then.

明天我將會在學校見到愛麗絲，到時我會給她這個消息。

▶ I **will be getting** dinner ready when the guests arrive.

當客人到達時，我將正好把晚餐準備好。

▶ We **will be sleeping** by the time you arrive home. 你回來的時候，我們將都在睡覺。

▶ **We will be stopping** at Cherry Park if we travel south.

如果我們往南走，我們會在櫻桃公園停留一下。

▶ At four o'clock tomorrow, we **will be** happily **swimming** in the sea.

明天四點的時候，我們將正在海裡快樂地游泳。

▶ What **will** you **be doing** at five o'clock? 你在五點時將會在做什麼？

▶ The airplane **will be flying** over the Atlantic Ocean by the time you read my letter.

當你讀我的這封信的時候，飛機將正在大西洋的上空飛行。

▶ He **will** probably **be having** dinner when you go there this evening.

當你今天晚上去那裡的時候，他將可能正在吃晚餐。

▶ He **will be working** on Tuesday. He is off on Monday. 星期二他將在工作，他星期一休假。

▶ **Will** he **be waiting** for us as usual tomorrow night? 明晚他將會照常在等我們嗎？

▶ He **will be passing** by my house on his way to school. 他上學途中將會經過我家。

▶ She **will be waiting** at the gate when I go back. 當我回去時，她將正在大門等。

▶ They **will be arriving** long before seven o'clock. 他們將早在七點以前就會到達。

(d) 請勿將未來簡單式與未來進行式混淆。切記，未來簡單式表達含「主觀意志」的
未來動作。

USAGE PRACTICE	
未來簡單式	未來進行式
▶ He **will not mow** the lawn. 他將不會除草。（他拒絕除草） ▶ I **will walk** home. 我將會走路回家。（我不想開車）	▶ He **will not be mowing** the lawn. 他將不會在除草。（因為他還有事情要做） ▶ I **will be walking** home. 我將會走路回家。（因為我沒有車）

小練習

請根據提示在空格中填入正確的未來進行式動詞。

1. My feet _____ (*ache*) in these shoes by the time I arrive home.

2. The troupe of dancers from Grace Ballet Academy _____ (*appear*) at the stadium

next week.

3. If you put some charcoal on the fire now, it _____ still _____ (*burn*) tomorrow morning.

4. He _____ (*carry*) the flag in the parade today. _____ you _____ (*take*) part in the parade, too?

5. We _____ (*not entertain*) any guests this evening, owing to a change of plans. Instead, we _____ (*camp*) in the back of the garden tonight.

6. By the end of this year, you _____ (*finish*) your course in Domestic Science.

7. My grandfather _____ (*celebrate*) his 60th birthday next year.

8. I _____ (*prepare*) new work for you to do after you have completed the project.

9. He _____ (*wear*) a red carnation in his buttonhole when he meets you at the railway station.

10. It is nearly six o'clock. People _____ (*wake*) up soon.

11. The whole class _____ (*pay*) a visit to the caves during the weekend. _____ some of the teachers _____ (*accompany*) us?

12. Do you think it _____ still _____ (*rain*) by the time we go home?

13. "One day, I _____ (*travel*) around the world." "I suppose you _____ (*dream*) about it till the day comes."

14. The train _____ (*depart*) from the station in a few minutes. In three hours, you _____ (*see*) your family again.

15. The boys _____ (*go*) to the National Archives this afternoon to do some research. They _____ (*not come*) home for lunch.

☞ 更多相關習題請見本章應用練習 Part 27～Part 30。

10-7 現在完成式

(a) 現在完成式主要是由「has/have + 過去分詞」構成。

USAGE PRACTICE		
肯定句	否定句	疑問句
▶ I **have lost** it.	→ I **haven't lost** it.	→ **Have** I **lost** it?

我已經把它弄丟了。	我沒有把它弄丟。	我已經把它弄丟了嗎？
▶ She **has come** here.	→ She **has not come** here.	→ **Has** she **come** here?
她已經來到這裡了。	她還沒有來到這裡。	她已經來到這裡了嗎？
▶ We **have seen** it.	→ We **have not seen** it.	→ **Have** we **seen** it?
我們已經看過它。	我們還沒看過它。	我們看過它了嗎？

(b) 現在完成式表示「從過去到現在為止已經完成的動作」，確切的完成時間並沒有被
提及，常與 already、recently 等副詞連用。

USAGE PRACTICE

▶ I **have repaired** the car. 我已經把車子修好了。

▶ There, I **have finished** my work. 喏，我已經完成我的工作了。

▶ I **have** already **made up** my mind about what to do. 我已經決定要做什麼事了。

▶ I **have** recently **started** collecting stamps. 我最近已經開始集郵了。

▶ **Have** you **watered** the plants? 你已經給植物澆水了嗎？

▶ He **has worked** out the sum. Won't you see if it's correct?

　他已經算出總數了。你要不要檢查是否正確？

▶ The child **has broken** the glass. 這個孩子已經把玻璃杯打破了。

▶ She **has** finally **decided** to go. 她終於決定要去了。

▶ She **has washed** the dishes. 她已經洗好碗了。

▶ She **has** already **gone** home. 她已經回家去了。

▶ She **has** recently **moved** to a new department. 她最近已經搬去一棟新的公寓了。

▶ They **have gone** to the market. 他們已經去市場了。

▶ **Have** they **made** all the arrangements? 他們已經全都安排妥當了嗎？

▶ The school bus **has not arrived** yet. 校車還沒有來。

(c) 現在完成式也可以表示「剛剛完成的動作」，常與 just、already、recently 等副詞
連用。

USAGE PRACTICE

▶ **Have** you just **finished** your homework? 你剛把家庭作業完成了嗎？

▶ He **has** recently **got** married. 他最近結婚了。

▶ She **has** just **gone** out. 她剛出門。

▶ She **has** just **had** her lunch. 她剛吃了午餐。

▶ They **have** just **bought** a refrigerator. 他們剛買了一個冰箱。

▶ They **have** just **informed** me of the change. 他們剛通知我這改變。

▶ We **have** just **returned** from a trip. 我們剛旅行回來。

▶ The baby **has** just **woke** up from his afternoon nap. 這個嬰兒午睡剛醒。

▶ It **has** just **started to** rain. 剛剛才開始下雨。

(d) 現在完成式可以表示「從過去到現在仍在持續進行的動作」，常與介系詞 for、since 等連用。since 後接表示「明確時間點」的名詞或片語，意思是「自從…」；而 for 則接表示「一段時間」的名詞或片語，意思是「持續了…的時間」。

USAGE PRACTICE

▶ I **have studied** in this school for many years. 我已經在這所學校就讀很多年了。

▶ He **has known** her for more than three years. 他已經認識她三年多了。

▶ He **hasn't come** here for a long time. 他已經有好一段時間不曾來這裡了。

▶ He **hasn't seen** her for two years. 他已經兩年沒見到她了。

▶ My grandfather **has been** ill for more than two weeks. 我的祖父已病了兩個多星期了。

▶ She **has locked** herself in the room for more than an hour.

她已經把自己鎖在房間內一個多小時了。

▶ They **have not written** to each other for a year. 他們彼此沒有書信往來已經有一年了。

▶ They **have lived** there for several years. 他們已經在那裡住了好幾年。

▶ The train **has been** in the station for more than an hour. 火車已經停在車站一個多小時了。

▶ I **have waited** for you since eight in the morning. 我從早上八點起就一直在等你。

▶ I **have been** in the garden since seven o'clock. 從七點起我就一直在花園裡。

▶ She **hasn't been** there since Friday. 自從星期五起，她就不在那裡了。

▶ She **has not seen** him since Christmas. 自從耶誕節後，她就沒看過他了。

▶ They **have not written** to each other since last year. 從去年起，他們彼此就沒有書信往來。

 since 也可以作連接詞，引導副詞子句。

▶ He **has lived** with us since he was five years old. 他從五歲起就和我們住在一起。

基礎文法寶典❸
Essential English Usage & Grammar

▶ He **has lived** here since he was born. 從出生以來，他就一直住在這裡。

▶ She **has been** in her room since she came home. 從她回到家，她就一直待在自己的房間裡。

(e) 現在完成式也可以與 up to now、up to the present、so far 等表示「到現在為止」的片語連用。

<table>
<tr><td>**USAGE PRACTICE**</td></tr>
</table>

▶ I **haven't done** a single thing up to now. 到目前為止，我一件事都還沒做。

▶ Up to the present I **have met** him only twice. 到現在為止，我只見過他兩次。

▶ He **has not spoken** to me up to now. 到現在為止，他還沒和我說話。

▶ We **have made** no progress so far. 到目前為止，我們沒有一點進展。

▶ **Have** they **prepared** for the experiment so far? 到目前為止，他們為實驗做準備了嗎？

(f) 現在完成式可以表示「從過去到現在的經驗」，常與 never、yet、before、ever、the first time 等字詞連用。

<table>
<tr><td>**USAGE PRACTICE**</td></tr>
</table>

▶ I **have** never **been** to Europe. 我從來不曾去過歐洲。

▶ **Have** you ever **been** to Paris? 你去過巴黎嗎？

▶ I **have seen** the film before. 我以前看過這部影片了。

▶ This will be the first time that I **have visited** a historic site. 這將是我第一次參訪古蹟。

▶ **Have** you ever **tried** to cook it in another way? 你曾經試過用另外一種方式烹調它嗎？

▶ He **has not met** her before. 他以前不曾遇見她。

▶ This is the first time that he **has driven** a car. 這是他第一次開車。

▶ He **has** never **seen** such an animal before. 他以前從未見過這樣的動物。

▶ They **have** never **come** here before. 以前他們從來不曾到過這裡。

(g) 句子中提到確切的過去時間時，動詞要用過去簡單式；沒提及特定的時間時，則用現在完成式。

USAGE PRACTICE	
現在完成式	過去簡單式

- I **have seen** her already.

  我已經看過她了。

- They **have gone** to the seaside.

  他們已經去海邊了。

- He **has locked** the door.

  他已經鎖門了。

- He **has** already **mailed** the letter.

  他已經把這封信寄出去了。

- He **has taught** us for six years.

  他已經教了我們六年。（現在仍然在教我們）

- She **has read** the book.

  她已經讀過這本書。

- I **saw** her a month ago.

  我一個月前看到她。

- They **went** to the seaside yesterday.

  他們昨天去了海邊。

- He **locked** the door an hour ago.

  他一個小時前鎖了門。

- He **mailed** the letter yesterday.

  他昨天把這封信寄了出去。

- He **taught** us for six years.

  他教了我們六年。（現在不教我們了）

- She **read** the book last night.

  她昨晚讀了這本書。

- I **have seen** it before. I **saw** it when I went there last year.

  我從前曾經看過它，去年我去那裡的時候就看見了它。

- I **have read** the book. I **read** it a week ago.

  我已經讀過這本書了，我是一週前讀的。

- He **has gone** to Atlanta. He **went** there on Tuesday.

  他已經去亞特蘭大了，他是在星期二去的。

- He **has not gone** to school all week. He **did not go** to school yesterday.

  他整整一週都不曾上學，他昨天也沒上學。

- They **have had** their dinner. They **had** their dinner at 8 o'clock.

  他們已經吃過晚餐了，他們是在八點吃的。

 有時候，該用現在完成式或過去簡單式是個難題，特別是在長句中。

- Last week just before we **went** on fishing, he **came** to our house and **asked** if he could join us. 上星期就在我們出發要去釣魚之前，他來到我們家並問他是否可以加入我們。

  （動詞用過去簡單式而非現在完成式）

- Yesterday while I was going to school, I **saw** Mary and her brother waiting for the bus.

  昨天正當我去上學的時候，我看見瑪莉和她的弟弟在等公車。

  （動詞用過去簡單式而非現在完成式）

(h) 在表示「現在某一時間範圍之內完成的動作」可以用現在完成式，超過該時間範圍就必須用過去簡單式。

USAGE PRACTICE

▶ I **have talked** to him this morning. 今天早上我已經和他談過話了。（現在仍然是早上。）

▶ I talked to him this morning. 今天早上我和他講過話。（現在已經不是早上了。）

▶ We **have been** there this afternoon. 今天下午我們一直都在那裡。（現在仍然是下午。）

▶ We **went** there this afternoon. 今天下午我們去了那裡。（現在已經不是下午了。）

小 練 習

請根據提示在空格中填入正確的現在完成式動詞。

1. "What _____ (*happen*)? _____ he _____ (*hurt*) himself?"

2. _____ you _____ (*tell*) your mother about it?

3. They _____ already _____ (*send*) in their subscriptions for the magazines.

4. He _____ (*not eat*) breakfast yet.

5. Her grandfather _____ just _____ (*make*) a will. _____ she _____ (*hear*) about it?

6. The plumber _____ (*be*) here for a while already, but he _____ (*not start*) on his work yet. He says that he _____ (*forget*) to bring a few tools.

7. Do you know who _____ (*buy*) the house?

8. I _____ (*have*) an argument with him over this issue.

9. The child _____ (*tear*) his trousers on the fence. He _____ (*scratch*) himself, too.

10. The gardener _____ (*wash*) the hutch and _____ (*put*) the rabbits back into it. _____ you _____ (*see*) them yet?

11. I hear the old man _____ (*win*) first prize in the lottery. _____ you _____ (*hear*) anything about it? It _____ (*be*) a long time since he visited us a few months ago.

☞ 更多相關習題請見本章應用練習 Part 31～Part 40。

10-8 過去完成式

(a) 過去完成式主要是由「had + 過去分詞」構成。

USAGE PRACTICE		
肯定句	否定句	疑問句
▶ I **had washed**.	→ I **had not washed**.	→ **Had** I **washed**?
我已經洗過了。	我還沒洗過。	我已經洗過了嗎？
▶ She **had eaten**.	→ She **had not eaten**.	→ **Had** she **eaten**?
她已經吃過了。	她還沒吃過。	她已經吃過了嗎？
▶ He **had run**.	→ He **had not run**.	→ **Had** he **run**?
他已經跑了。	他還沒跑。	他已經跑了嗎？
▶ They **had finished** it.	→ They **had not finished** it.	→ **Had** they **finished** it?
他們已經完成了。	他們還沒完成。	他們已經完成了嗎？

(b) 過去完成式可以用來表示「過去兩個動作中先發生者」，常與連接詞 when、before、after 或 just as 連用。

USAGE PRACTICE
▶ I read the book after I **had finished** my homework. 我做完家庭作業後，我讀了這本書。
▶ I **had** just **finished** writing the letter when he came in. 當他進來時，我剛剛寫完信。
▶ After he **had eaten** the food, he felt sick. 吃過食物後，他覺得不舒服。
▶ He **had arrived** just as I was leaving my house. 正當我要離開家時，他們已經到了。
▶ We **had eaten** dinner when she came home. 當她回家時，我們已經吃完晚餐了。
▶ The thieves **had escaped** when the police arrived. 當警方到達時，小偷已經逃走了。
▶ We **had cooked** dinner before she came home. 在她回家以前，我們已經煮好晚餐了。
▶ We **had heard** the news before we set out for work.
在我們出發去工作之前，我們已經聽到這個消息。
▶ They **had locked** the door before they left. 在離開之前，他們已經把門鎖好。
▶ They went off after they **had waited** for about thirty minutes.
等了大約三十分鐘後，他們就離開了。
▶ After they **had gone**, she crept out of her hiding place. 他們離去之後，她爬出她的藏身之處。
▶ The bus **had gone** when we reached the bus stop. 當我們到達公車站時，公車已經走了。

(c) 過去完成式也可以表示「某一動作在過去某一時間已經完成」。

USAGE PRACTICE

▶ By the time the firefighters came, the building **had burned** down.

消防隊員來的時候，這棟大樓已經燒毀了。

▶ By the time we reached there, the train **had left**. 我們抵達那裡的時候，火車已經開走了。

▶ By the time we came home, the children **had fallen** asleep.

我們回到家時，孩子們都已睡著了。

▶ The girls **had gone** by the time we arrived. 我們到達的時候，女孩們就已經離開了。

▶ By the time he was six, he **had learned** how to swim. 他六歲的時候，就已經學會游泳了。

▶ He **had recovered** from his illness by Wednesday. 在星期三之前，他的病就好了。

▶ By twelve o'clock, he **had** already **finished** the job. 在十二點之前，他就已經完成這工作了。

▶ They **had finished** their dinner by eight o'clock. 在八點之前，他們就已經吃完晚餐了。

▶ They **had gone** home by one o'clock. 在一點之前，他們就已經回家了。

(d) 直接引句改成間接引句時，要將現在完成式或過去簡單式改為過去完成式。

USAGE PRACTICE

▶ He said, "I have lost my watch." 他說：「我的手錶掉了。」（直接引句）

  → He said that he **had lost** his watch. 他說他的手錶掉了。（間接引句）

▶ You said, "They have gone to the movies." 你說：「他們已經去看電影了。」（直接引句）

  → You said that they **had gone** to the movies. 你說他們已經去看電影了。（間接引句）

▶ She said, "I have already finished my work." 她說：「我已經完成我的工作了。」（直接引句）

  → She said that she **had** already **finished** her work.

    她說她已經完成她的工作了。（間接引句）

▶ "He has finished his work," she said. 「他已經完成他的工作了。」她說。（直接引句）

  → She said that he **had finished** his work. 她說他已經完成他的工作了。（間接引句）

▶ "Where did you go?" he asked. 「你去了哪裡？」他問。（直接引句）

  → He asked where I **had gone**. 他問我去了哪裡。（間接引句）

▶ "I have done my work," I said. 「我已經做了我的工作。」我說。（直接引句）

  → I said that I **had done** my work. 我說我已經做了我的工作。（間接引句）

▶ "I locked the door myself," she said. 「我自己鎖門了。」她說。(直接引句)

　　→ She said that she **had locked** the door herself. 她說她自己已經鎖門了。(間接引句)

(e) hope、expect、think、intend、want 等動詞用過去完成式時，表示「過去期望或想做，但沒做或沒實現的事」。

USAGE PRACTICE

▶ We **had hoped** that she would be able to come. 我們原本希望她會能來。

▶ He **had planned** to wash the car, but the rain did the work for him.

　他原本計畫要洗車，但是雨水幫他洗了。

▶ I **had thought** of visiting you, but there just wasn't time. 我原本想要拜訪你，但就是沒有時間。

▶ They **had expected** him to return by nine. 他們原先預期他能在九點前回來。

▶ We **had expected** him to come. 我們本來期望他會來的。

請根據提示在空格中填入正確的過去完成式動詞。

1. He told us that they ＿＿＿＿＿＿ just ＿＿＿＿＿＿ (*see*) the film.

2. After they ＿＿＿＿＿＿ (*be*) to the concert, they went to a party.

3. When she ＿＿＿＿＿＿ (*take*) her medicine, she went to bed.

4. By completing the race in four minutes, he ＿＿＿＿＿＿ (*break*) the world record.

5. He ＿＿＿＿＿＿ (*employ*) a lawyer to fight the case for him.

6. ＿＿＿＿＿＿ the accident ＿＿＿＿＿＿ (*happen*) before then?

7. By three o'clock, he ＿＿＿＿＿＿ (*memorize*) all his lines for the play.

8. The teacher ＿＿＿＿＿＿ (*take*) away all their storybooks before they could protest.

9. After he ＿＿＿＿＿＿ (*be*) sick for two weeks, he was very weak.

10. He said that he ＿＿＿＿＿＿ (*know*) the truth all along.

11. At the age of five, he ＿＿＿＿＿＿ (*learn*) to read and write.

12. His handwriting ＿＿＿＿＿＿ (*go*) from bad to worse since he came back from his holidays.

13. When he ＿＿＿＿＿＿ (*hammer*) a nail into the wall, he hung up the picture.

☞ 更多相關習題請見本章應用練習 Part 41～Part 45。

10-9 未來完成式

(a) 未來完成式主要是由「will + have + 過去分詞」構成。

USAGE PRACTICE		
肯定句	否定句	疑問句
▶ The show **will have finished** by five. 五點前，這表演將已經結束。	→ The show **will not have finished** by five. 五點前，這表演將還沒結束。	→ **Will** the show **have finished** by five? 五點前，這表演將已結束了嗎？

(b) 未來完成式表示「在未來某一明確時間點已經完成的動作」，常與時間副詞或片語連用。

USAGE PRACTICE
▶ I **will have completed** my course in three years. 三年之內，我將已經完成我的課程。
▶ You **will have grown** quite tall in four years. 四年內，你將已經長得相當高了。
▶ In an hour, he **will have left** the house. 在一個小時內，他將已經離開這房子。
▶ In a year he **will have graduated** from the college. 一年內，他將已經大學畢業。
▶ The boys **will have had** their dinner by half past seven. 七點半前，這些男孩將已吃過晚飯。
▶ By ten o'clock, the men **will have** all **gone** home. 十點前，這些男人全部都將已回家。
▶ She **will have saved** a thousand dollars by the end of this year. 今年年底前，她將已經存了一千元。
▶ By tomorrow, everyone **will have heard** the news. 明天之前，每一個人都將已經聽到這個消息。
▶ The bomb **will have exploded** by now. 此刻炸彈將已經爆炸。
▶ The concert **will have started** by then, won't it? 到那時候，音樂會將已經開始了，不是嗎？

(c) 未來完成式表示「在未來某一動作前已經完成的動作」，常與時間副詞或片語連用。

USAGE PRACTICE
▶ She **will have gone** by the time you reach there. 你到達這裡的時候，她將已經離去。

▶ The show **will have started** by the time we get there. 我們到那裡時，表演將已經開始。

▶ I **will have finished** by the time he arrives. 他到達時，我將會已經完成。

▶ The rain **won't have stopped** by the time the show ends. 表演結束時，雨將還不會停。

(d) 未來完成式表示「將持續到未來某一時間（且可能還會持續下去）的動作或狀態」，常與時間副詞或片語連用。

USAGE PRACTICE

▶ She **will have worked** there for ten years by July. 七月前，她將已經在那裡工作十年了。

(e) 未來完成式可以用來表示「對未來的推測」。

USAGE PRACTICE

▶ We're very late; the others will have gone when we arrive.

我們遲到很久；當我們抵達的時候其他人將會已經離開了。

▶ He **will have realized** how wrong he was about you.

他將會了解他過去對你的誤解有多深。

▶ You **will have noticed** from my speech how important this subject really is.

你會從我的演講中注意到這個主題有多重要。

▶ She is your best friend. She **will have told** you the news.

她是你最要好的朋友，她將會告訴你這消息。

小練習

請根據提示在空格中填入正確的未來完成式動詞。

1. I hope the goods _____ (*reach*) our customers by now.

2. In an hour, I _____ (*inform*) my parents of the change in my plans.

3. By the time we reach the port, we _____ (*travel*) 300 kilometers.

4. The helicopter _____ (*be*) on its way to help the stranded soldiers by now.

5. They _____ (*see*) the advertisement in the newspaper by tomorrow morning.

6. You can dry the clothes later. The sun _____ (*come*) out by then.

7. Someone on the train _____ (*find*) the package by now.

8. I _____ (*burn*) all my old notebooks in a few minutes.

9. We _____ (*switch*) off all the lights at twelve midnight.

10. Before you know it, she _____ (*persuade*) him to take her to the carnival.

11. When we reach the first station, we _____ (*climb*) three hundred meters above sea level.

12. The police _____ (*hear*) of the theft by this time.

13. When you get the message, she _____ (*move*) to another lodging house.

14. When the sailors reach Midway Island, they _____ (*sail*) halfway around the world.

15. At the rate you are going, you _____ (*use*) up all your energy before the big day comes.

16. My brother _____ (*graduate*) from college by the time I am twenty years old.

17. By next term, all of us _____ (*learn*) how to appreciate good literature.

18. I _____ (*write*) four letters by the time he comes back.

19. When I come back, he probably _____ (*eat*) all the groundnuts in the can.

20. By tomorrow, the news _____ (*spread*) to every part of the village.

21. Mr. Lester _____ (*work*) here for ten years when April comes.

22. My friends _____ (*see*) everything of interest in my town within two hours.

☞ 更多相關習題請見本章應用練習 Part 46～Part 47。

10-10 現在完成進行式

(a) 現在完成進行式主要是由「have/has + been + 現在分詞」構成，強調「未被中斷的動作的持續性」。

USAGE PRACTICE		
肯定句	否定句	疑問句
▶ I **have been singing**.	→ I **have not been singing**.	→ **Have** I **been singing**?
我一直在唱歌。	我沒有一直在唱歌。	我一直在唱歌嗎？
▶ She **has been sewing**.	→ She **has not been sewing**.	→ **Has** she **been sewing**?
她一直在縫衣服。	她沒有一直在縫衣服。	她一直在縫衣服嗎？

(b) 現在完成進行式表示「一個從過去開始、到目前仍然持續進行或剛剛停止的動作」，
常與 for、since 引導的片語、子句或時間副詞連用。

USAGE PRACTICE

▶ I **have been reading** since three o'clock this afternoon.

自從今天下午三點起，我就一直在看書。

▶ I **have been waiting** here for two hours. 我已經一直在這裡等了兩個小時。

▶ What **have** you **been doing** all morning? 你整個上午一直在做什麼？

▶ Your friends **have been waiting** for you since three o'clock.

你的朋友從三點起就一直在等你。

▶ He **has been resting** in the room for more than two hours.

他已在房間裡休息了兩個多小時了。

▶ He **has been sleeping** since he came back from the office.

自他從辦公室回來，就一直在睡覺。

▶ Mr. White **has been working** with the company for many years.

懷特先生一直在這家公司工作了許多年。

▶ She **has been crying** for a long time. 她一直哭了好久。

▶ She **has not been attending** the meetings lately. 最近她一直沒參加會議。

▶ **Have** they **been living** here for many years? 他們一直住在這裡許多年了嗎？

▶ They **have been studying** since one o'clock. 自從一點起，他們就一直在讀書。

▶ It **hasn't been working** since last week. 自從上個星期起，它就一直沒有在運轉。

▶ It **has been raining** very heavily since this morning. 從今天早上起，雨就一直下得很大。

▶ The dog **has been barking** the whole evening. 這隻狗整個晚上一直在吠叫。

(c) 當強調「動作持續進行而未中斷」時，用現在完成進行式；當強調「一個完成的
動作」，則用現在完成式。

USAGE PRACTICE

現在完成式	現在完成進行式
▶ I **have spoken** to him about the matter. 我已經跟他講過這件事了。	▶ I **have been speaking** to him about the matter. 我一直在跟他講這件事。

▶ I **have done** my homework.

我已經做完功課了。

▶ I **have read** this book.

我已經讀過這本書了。

▶ How long **have** you **sat** here?

你在這裡坐了多久？

▶ What **have** you **done** so far?

到目前為止你做了什麼？

▶ **Have** you already **tidied** your room?

你已經打掃好你的房間了嗎？

▶ **Have** you **slept** well?

你睡得好嗎？

▶ He **has** just **rung** the bell.

他剛剛按了鈴。

▶ He **has** just **eaten**.

他剛剛吃過了。

▶ He **has not written** to me.

他不曾寫信給我。

▶ They **have discussed** the matter.

他們已經討論過這件事了。

▶ They **have walked** over from that farm.

他們已經從那個農場走過來。

▶ We **have worked** for two hours.

我們已經工作兩小時了。

▶ The doorbell **has rung** twice.

門鈴已經響了兩次。

▶ I **have been doing** my homework since this afternoon. 從今天下午我就一直在做功課。

▶ I **have been reading** this book.

我一直在讀這本書。

▶ How long **have** you **been sitting** here?

你一直在這裡坐了多久？

▶ What **have** you **been doing** all this time?

你這陣子一直在做些什麼事呢？

▶ **Have** you **been tidying** your room since you woke up?

自從起床後，你就一直在打掃你的房間嗎？

▶ **Have** you **been sleeping** while I was out?

我外出時，你一直在睡覺嗎？

▶ He **has been ringing** the bell for more than ten minutes. 他一直按鈴按了十多分鐘。

▶ He **has been eating** for half an hour.

他已經吃了半小時了。

▶ He **has not been writing** to me since we quarreled.

自從我們吵架後，他一直不曾寫信給我。

▶ They **have been discussing** the matter for two hours.

他們一直在討論這件事已經兩小時了。

▶ They **have been walking** for more than an hour. 他們一直走了一個多小時。

▶ We **have been working** for two hours.

我們一直工作了兩小時。

▶ The doorbell **has been ringing** for the past five minutes.

在過去五分鐘裡，門鈴一直在響。

(d) 不能使用進行式的動詞，同樣也不能使用完成進行式，只能用完成式。

 但是當這類動詞用在其他的意思時，有些就可以用現在完成進行式。

▶ I **have been hearing** all sorts of stories about him. 我一直聽到關於他的種種故事。

▶ She **has been thinking** about him all day. 她整天一直在想他。

▶ He **has been feeling** awful all morning. 他一整個早上一直覺得不舒服。

請根據提示在空格中填入正確的現在完成進行式動詞。

1. Why don't you answer the door bell? It _____ (*ring*) for a long time.

2. They _____ (*not write*) to each other since they quarreled a month ago.

3. She _____ (*wait*) for him since it started getting dark.

4. The committee _____ (*call*) meetings too often.

5. Henry _____ (*study*) in Main City for the past couple of years.

6. I _____ (*try*) to solve this mathematical problem for the past fifteen minutes.

7. How long _____ you _____ (*sit*) by the roadside?

8. _____ the children _____ (*behave*) themselves since Mother went to the market?

9. They _____ (*bully*) us for a long time. It's time someone taught them a lesson.

10. I _____ (*look*) for you everywhere. What _____ you _____ (*do*) all this while?

11. The water _____ (*boil*) for several minutes. _____ you _____ (*not wait*) for the water to make tea?

☞ 更多相關習題請見本章應用練習 Part 48～Part 56。

10-11 過去完成進行式

(a) 過去完成進行式主要是由「had + been + 現在分詞」構成。

USAGE PRACTICE		
肯定句	否定句	疑問句
▶ She **had been reading**.	→ She **had not been reading**.	→ **Had** she **been reading**?
她一直在讀書。	她沒有一直在讀書。	她一直在讀書嗎？

(b) 過去完成式和過去完成進行式都用來表示「過去發生的動作」，但是過去完成進行式更強調「動作的持續進行」，常與表示時間的片語或副詞子句連用。

USAGE PRACTICE
▶ He **had been guarding** the camp last night.　昨晚他一直看守這個營地。
▶ He **had been lying** on the floor for an hour before they found him.
在他們找到他之前，他已經一直躺在地上一個小時了。
▶ He **had been working** in the office for five years before he was promoted.
在他升遷前，他已經一直在這辦公室工作五年了。
▶ Mr. Jones **had been living** in Ivy Square for three years when he left.
當瓊斯先生離開的時候，他已經一直住在長春藤廣場三年了。
▶ **Had** she **been working** hard on the project?　她一直努力在做這案子嗎？
▶ There were dark shadows under her eyes. **Hadn't** she **been sleeping** well?
她有黑眼圈。她一直沒睡好嗎？
▶ We **had** just **been telling** him about the robbery in the neighborhood.
我們剛剛一直跟他講鄰近地區的那件搶案。
▶ We **had been expecting** you since this morning.　我們從今天早上就已經一直在等你們。
▶ After they **had been walking** for about twenty minutes, they decided to have a rest.
在他們已經一直走了大約二十分鐘後，他們決定要休息一下。
▶ They **had been waiting** for you for a long time.　他們已經一直等待你們好一段時間。
▶ They **had been studying** together for nine years.　他們一直一起讀書九年了。

> The water **had been boiling** for some time before she noticed it.

在她注意到之前，這水已經一直沸騰了一段時間。

(c) 直接引句改成間接引句時，可以用過去完成進行式代替現在完成進行式或過去進行式。

USAGE PRACTICE

> "I have been tidying up my room," she said.

「我已經一直在整理我的房間了。」她說。（直接引句）

→ She said that she **had been tidying up** her room.

她說她已經一直在整理她的房間了。（間接引句）

> "You have been looking for the wrong man," he said. 「你一直找錯人。」他說。（直接引句）

→ He said that I **had been looking for** the wrong man. 他說我一直找錯人。（間接引句）

> "Has she been crying?" I asked. 「她一直都在哭嗎？」我問。（直接引句）

→ I asked whether she **had been crying**. 我問是否她一直在哭。（間接引句）

> "I have been waiting for you for an hour," he told me.

「我一直在等你已經有一個小時了。」他告訴我。（直接引句）

→ He told me that he **had been waiting** for me for an hour.

他告訴我，他一直在等我已經有一個小時了。（間接引句）

> They replied, "We have been discussing the problem the whole afternoon."

他們回答說：「我們整個下午已經一直在討論這個問題了。」（直接引句）

→ They replied that they **had been discussing** the problem the whole afternoon.

他們回答說他們整個下午已經一直在討論那個問題了。（間接引句）

> She said, "I was reading in my room." 她說：「我正在我的房間讀書。」（直接引句）

→ She said that she **had been reading** in her room.

她說她一直在她的房間讀書。（間接引句）

> "Where **have** you **been playing**?" he asked the boys.

「你們一直在哪裡玩？」他問男孩們。（直接引句）

→ He asked the boys where they **had been playing**. 他問男孩們一直在哪裡玩。（間接引句）

> They said, "We have been fishing here for two hours."

他們說：「我們一直在這裡釣魚兩小時了。」（直接引句）

基礎文法寶典 **③**
Essential English Usage & Grammar

> → They said that they **had been fishing** there for two hours.
>
> 他們說他們一直在那裡釣魚兩小時了。(間接引句)

小練習

請根據提示在空格中填入正確的過去完成進行式動詞。

1. They _____ (*borrow*) books from that library since they moved into the neighborhood.

2. She _____ (*lie*) awake for more than three hours.

3. Where _____ he _____ (*hide*) all this time?

4. The can of petrol _____ (*leak*) as he carried it to the car.

5. The telephone _____ (*ring*) for several minutes before he answered it.

6. We _____ (*count*) the votes since last night.

7. It _____ (*rain*) during the match yesterday.

8. After he _____ (*work*) for two hours in the sun, he felt very tired.

9. We asked her whether she _____ (*go*) to the seaside lately.

10. They _____ (*not listen*) to the music at all.

11. She was very angry as she _____ (*wait*) for us all yesterday afternoon.

12. They said that they _____ (*watch*) television when the thief entered.

13. He was panting for breath after he _____ (*climb*) the hill for about an hour.

14. They _____ (*do*) their homework when I walked into the room.

15. He _____ (*bathe*) before the visitors came.

16. The athlete _____ (*run*) around the track when lightning struck him.

☞ 更多相關習題請見本章應用練習 Part 57～Part 59。

10-12 未來完成進行式

(a) 未來完成進行式主要是由「will + have + been + 現在分詞」構成，表示「未來將會繼續進行的動作」，也常與表示時間的片語連用。

USAGE PRACTICE

▶ I **will have been working** in this office for ten years by Christmas (and I will continue to work here). 到耶誕節，我將已經在這辦公室工作十年了。(而且我將會繼續在這裡工作)

► By evening, they **will have been playing** for four hours (and they will probably continue to play). 到傍晚，他們將已經玩了四個小時。（而且他們可能會繼續玩）

Chapter 10　應用練習

PART 1

請根據提示在空格中填入正確的現在簡單式動詞。

1. The sun _____ (*give*) us warmth and light. It _____ (*kill*) germs, too.

2. The dog _____ (*obey*) every word its master _____ (*say*).

3. Light _____ (*travel*) in a straight line.

4. He always _____ (*hurry*) through his meals. I often _____ (*tell*) him it _____ (*be*) bad, but he never _____ (*listen*) to me.

5. The train normally _____ (*reach*) the station on time.

6. My father _____ (*not work*) on Sundays. He usually _____ (*go*) fishing with some of his colleagues.

7. The ship _____ (*set*) sail for Sydney on the tenth of May.

8. Those shelves _____ (*clean*) every week. The shopkeeper's assistant usually _____ (*do*) the work.

9. It all _____ (*depend*) on whether she _____ (*agree*) to it or not.

10. One of my uncles _____ (*work*) in a toy factory. He often _____ (*bring*) home toys for my sister and me.

11. This type of glass _____ (*not break*) easily. It _____ (*be*) suitable for making windshields.

12. That machine _____ (*seem*) to work quite well. There _____ (*be*) nothing wrong with it.

13. When the curtain _____ (*rise*), the king is sitting on the throne. A servant _____ (*come*) in and _____ (*bow*) low before him.

14. _____ you _____ (*know*) the way to his house? You _____ (*live*) near him, don't you?

15. We _____ (*spend*) our holidays by the seaside every year. The sea air _____ (*do*) us

good.

16. The bus _____ (*leave*) school punctually at 8 a.m. It _____ (*not wait*) for latecomers.

17. "Andy _____ (*swing*) his racket and _____ (*send*) the shuttlecock over the net. Jack _____ (*give*) a smash with his racket, but the shuttlecock _____ (*land*) outside the line..."

PART 2

請根據提示在空格中填入正確的現在簡單式動詞。

1. William _____ (*get*) up at seven in the morning.

2. It _____ (*not matter*) whether she _____ (*go*) there or not.

3. That garden table _____ (*be*) made of marble.

4. She usually _____ (*leave*) for work at eight o'clock.

5. The sun _____ (*rise*) in the east and _____ (*set*) in the west.

6. She _____ (*do*) her homework and _____ (*study*) until it _____ (*be*) ten o'clock.

7. "Here it _____ (*come*)!" he shouted. "_____ it _____ (*not look*) beautiful?"

8. He often _____ (*go*) to society meetings in the afternoon and _____ (*return*) at six o'clock.

9. When the cock _____ (*crow*) early in the morning, it _____ (*be*) time for everyone to get up.

10. He _____ (*believe*) every word she _____ (*say*).

11. Her house _____ (*be*) rather difficult to find unless one _____ (*know*) the area well.

12. The airplane _____ (*leave*) the airport at 9 p.m. and _____ (*reach*) its destination in four hours.

13. John _____ (*study*) very hard. He _____ (*hope*) to get a scholarship, and he _____ (*know*) that only the best students _____ (*get*) them.

14. The ship _____ (*not stop*) at the port but _____ (*sail*) on until it _____ (*reach*) Singapore.

15. Whenever she _____ (*get*) excited, she _____ (*jump*) up and down and _____ (*clap*) her hands.

16. Susan _____ (*be*) a very careless girl and always _____ (*misplace*) her things. When

she _____ (*find*) something missing, she _____ (*get*) upset and _____ (*turn*) the whole house upside down searching for it.

PART 3

請根據提示在空格中填入正確的現在簡單式動詞。

1. The earth _____ (*rotate*) on its own axis and it also _____ (*revolve*) around the sun.

2. When you _____ (*reach*) your destination, _____ (*send*) us an email.

3. The ship _____ (*leave*) Lighthouse Island on Wednesday and _____ (*arrive*) at Port Haven on Friday.

4. "Billy _____ (*pass*) the ball to the right. The center forward _____ (*rush*) in and _____ (*intercept*) the ball. He _____ (*throw*) the ball but Peter _____ (*dash*) forward and _____ (*grab*) it..."

5. He _____ (*select*) a suitable piece of wood and _____ (*carve*) it till it _____ (*resemble*) a bowl in shape. Then, he _____ (*polish*) it till it _____ (*be*) smooth.

6. The Ganges _____ (*flow*) down the Himalayas and _____ (*meander*) its way toward the sea.

7. My brother often _____ (*play*) football in the evening and _____ (*not come*) home until seven o'clock. Immediately after he _____ (*return*), he _____ (*take*) a bath and _____ (*change*) into clean clothes.

8. That man _____ (*deliver*) eggs to our house every week. Sometimes he _____ (*bring*) our groceries, too. If we _____ (*be*) not at home when he _____ (*come*), he _____ (*leave*) the things with our neighbors.

9. The last bus _____ (*leave*) at five o'clock and _____ (*reach*) our hometown at ten o'clock. If we _____ (*not hurry*), we may not be able to catch it.

10. When he _____ (*come*) and _____ (*inquire*) for me, _____ (*tell*) him I _____ (*be*) not at home. I _____ (*not want*) to see him.

11. Nowadays, a lot of children _____ (*know*) how to swim. Some _____ (*take*) lessons while others _____ (*learn*) by themselves.

12. She _____ (*dislike*) traveling by air as it _____ (*give*) her a headache. She _____ (*prefer*) to travel by sea.

13. We _____ (*fasten*) our seat belts and _____ (*wait*) for the plane to take off. Soon,

the plane _____ (*leave*) the ground and smoothly _____ (*rise*) into the sky.

14. First, the cook _____ (*collect*) all the utensils and _____ (*measure*) out all the ingredients that she _____ (*need*). Then, she _____ (*begin*) to mix the ingredients together. She _____ (*work*) quickly, and before long, the cake _____ (*be*) in the oven.

15. The commentator spoke excitedly, "David _____ (*swing*) a left hook at Sam, but Sam _____ (*dodge*). Then Sam _____ (*seize*) an opportunity and _____ (*deliver*) a hard one to David's jaw..."

16. The boys _____ (*stop*) at Crown Hill on the way home. Then, they _____ (*move*) on to Rainbow Valley, and _____ (*visit*) the places of interest there before they _____ (*set*) off for home.

PART 4

請根據提示在空格中填入正確的現在簡單式動詞。

1. He always _____ (*sleep*) late on Sundays. That _____ (*be*) because he _____ (*work*) late every Saturday night.

2. My father _____ (*travel*) around a lot in his job. He often _____ (*send*) home souvenirs of the places he _____ (*go*) to.

3. Working hours _____ (*start*) at half past eight and _____ (*end*) at five in the afternoon.

4. The scale at the side of the cylinder _____ (*show*) the volume and _____ (*mark*) it in cubic centimeters.

5. The rest of the boys _____ (*seem*) to have disappeared. It _____ (*look*) as though we have to do the work ourselves.

6. The fishermen _____ (*get*) up before the sun _____ (*rise*).

7. At that point, the road _____ (*branch*) to the left. It _____ (*follow*) the river for some distance.

8. That girl _____ (*remind*) me of a friend of mine who _____ (*work*) in a pharmacy.

9. The buttons on this shirt always _____ (*come*) off.

10. He _____ (*say*) that oranges _____ (*cost*) more than apples.

11. They _____ (*build*) a shelter for spectators on the field in case it _____ (*rain*) during

the games.

12. We usually _____ (*clean*) the kitchen once a week. It _____ (*need*) cleaning now.

13. This river _____ (*flow*) from the mountains, and _____ (*pass*) through the town before it _____ (*reach*) the sea.

14. Those jugs _____ (*crack*) easily. They _____ (*be*) different from this type.

15. This line _____ (*mark*) the highest level of the sea when high tide _____ (*come*).

16. Find a piece of rope which _____ (*reach*) to the ground floor and which _____ (*be*) thick enough to support your weight.

17. The fire _____ (*burn*) all night. It _____ (*last*) till the morning.

18. He _____ (*expect*) us to agree to whatever he _____ (*recommend*), but I _____ (*not intend*) to do so this time.

19. She _____ (*think*) she _____ (*know*) the solution to every problem, but this time she _____ (*find*) herself stumped.

20. The path _____ (*fork*) off near Woodland Downs. The left path _____ (*lead*) to the village, but the right one _____ (*take*) you nowhere.

PART 5

請根據提示在空格中填入正確的過去簡單式動詞。

1. In spite of the heat, the soldiers _____ (*march*) quickly. Soon, they _____ (*reach*) the top of the hill where they _____ (*have*) a rest. Then, they _____ (*continue*) their march.

2. He _____ (*dive*) into the river and _____ (*swim*) quickly across it.

3. He _____ (*remove*) his coat and _____ (*hang*) it on a nail. He _____ (*sit*) down and _____ (*begin*) to take off his shoes.

4. They _____ (*celebrate*) their victory with a dinner at the Traveler's Inn. Everybody _____ (*be*) in a joyous mood and the celebration _____ (*last*) all night.

5. The rain _____ (*start*) to fall just as we _____ (*walk*) out of the house, so I _____ (*rush*) back for an umbrella.

6. She _____ (*study*) hard and therefore _____ (*do*) quite well in her examination.

7. I _____ (*walk*) up the garden path to the front door. Nobody _____ (*seem*) to be at home, but I _____ (*ring*) the bell anyway.

8. The old man _____ (*trip*) over a stone and _____ (*fall*) down on the road. A

passer-by _____ (*hurry*) to his aid.

9. Tongues of flame _____ (*leap*) out of the windows and soon the whole house _____

(*be*) on fire.

10. Early men _____ (*live*) in caves and _____ (*use*) crude stone tools.

11. He _____ (*spend*) a lot of money while he _____ (*be*) in Hawaii. He _____

(*buy*) gifts for the family and _____ (*visit*) many scenic spots.

12. My brother _____ (*come*) home late in the afternoon. He _____ (*have*) a bath,

_____ (*eat*) his lunch, and soon _____ (*go*) out again.

13. The basketball game _____ (*thrill*) the spectators. They _____ (*clap*) and

_____ (*cheer*) whenever a player _____ (*score*).

14. We _____ (*not talk*) long with each other as he _____ (*be*) in a hurry.

15. She _____ (*taste*) the soup and _____ (*begin*) to add more salt to it.

16. Mary _____ (*not understand*) what she was reading. She _____ (*find*) the contents

too difficult for her.

17. "_____ he _____ (*suffer*) much before he _____ (*die*)?" "No, it _____

(*be*) all over in a few minutes."

18. "_____ a porter _____ (*carry*) the bags for you?" "Yes, he did. I _____ (*tip*)

him a dollar for doing so."

19. They _____ (*tell*) me that they _____ (*go*) to a show last night. They _____

(*not enjoy*) it very much and _____ (*wish*) that they had stayed at home.

20. The child _____ (*run*) across the room, _____ (*open*) the door, and _____ (*go*)

out.

21. "_____ (*be*) you angry when they _____ (*fail*) to send you an invitation?" "No, I

_____ (*be not*)."

22. My father _____ (*come*) home from a very successful fishing trip last evening. He

_____ (*catch*) some big fish.

23. Thieves _____ (*break*) into the Smiths' house last night. The thieves _____ (*steal*) a

lot of money and jewelry. The Smiths _____ (*discover*) the theft only this morning.

24. She _____ (*feel*) ill after she had eaten the fruit. We _____ (*rush*) her to the doctor,

who _____ (*treat*) her.

PART 6

請根據提示在空格中填入正確的過去簡單式動詞。

1. He _____ (*take*) out a pencil, _____ (*tear*) a page from his diary, and _____ (*begin*) to write.

2. He _____ (*write*) down the address and _____ (*seal*) the envelope.

3. The driver _____ (*step*) hard on his brake, but the car _____ (*skid*) and _____ (*collide*) with an oncoming car.

4. She _____ (*practice*) every day until she _____ (*be*) adept at using the instrument.

5. You _____ (*see*) the man who _____ (*pass*) by just now, didn't you?

6. He _____ (*not turn*) on the radio as he _____ (*not want*) to be disturbed.

7. With a bang, the door _____ (*swing*) shut and the force of it _____ (*shake*) the old house.

8. The prisoners _____ (*bore*) a tunnel under the fence and _____ (*escape*) that way.

9. She _____ (*tidy*) up the room, _____ (*sweep*) the floor, and _____ (*go*) out.

10. You _____ (*remember*) to lock the door when you _____ (*come*) out, didn't you?

11. The dog _____ (*try*) to bite me, but I _____ (*kick*) it away.

12. They both _____ (*laugh*) till their sides _____ (*ache*).

13. After the meal, they _____ (*take*) a walk while she _____ (*wash*) the dishes.

14. "_____ you _____ (*sleep*) well last night?" they _____ (*inquire*).

15. The sun _____ (*become*) only a red glow as it _____ (*sink*) behind the hills.

16. A light _____ (*flicker*) in the darkness and a voice _____ (*whisper*), "Over here!"

17. They _____ (*travel*) for many days till they _____ (*reach*) the border of the country.

18. When Peter _____ (*start*) to climb up the hill, he _____ (*discover*) a cave hidden behind some creepers and bushes.

PART 7

請根據提示在空格中填入正確的未來簡單式動詞（限用 will）。

1. There are no clouds in the sky today. It _____ (*be*) a hot afternoon.

2. She has bought a lot of food at the supermarket. She _____ (*cook*) us something special tomorrow.

3. I _____ (*not forget*) to wish him "Happy Birthday" tomorrow.

4. _____ we _____ (go) home by taxi instead of by bus?

5. There is a good program on television tonight. We _____ (stay) at home to watch it.

6. The bell _____ (ring) any minute now. _____ we _____ (line) up on the field?

7. I _____ (write) a letter to tell him we are coming.

8. He has brought back a packet of seeds from Petals Nursery. When _____ you _____ (plant) them?

9. He _____ (help) me with my painting.

10. Both of them _____ (leave) the university this year. They told me that they _____ (do) post-graduate study in Europe.

11. How _____ you _____ (get) there when the road is closed to all traffic at nine o'clock?

12. The table is dirty. _____ you _____ (not wipe) it off?

13. The members _____ (contribute) money regularly to the society.

14. If you are sick, who _____ (take) care of the family? Your husband _____ (be) at work the whole day.

15. The plane _____ (leave) in an hour. You _____ (miss) it if you don't hurry.

16. We _____ (serve) lunch at eleven o'clock today, but I don't think that any of us _____ (be) very hungry then.

PART 8

請根據提示在空格中填入正確的未來簡單式動詞（限用 will）。

1. He _____ (meet) his uncle at the station at five o'clock.

2. _____ you _____ (push) the wheelbarrow into the shed?

3. When it is time to go home, the school bell _____ (ring).

4. My father _____ (go) on a tour of Europe next month. He _____ (be) back in April next year.

5. I _____ (ask) him to come here at once. It _____ (be) good for him to start at once.

6. If she is more patient, she _____ (*succeed*) in getting what she wants.

7. I _____ (*not vote*) for him for president again next time.

8. We _____ (*have*) a coffee break at three o'clock. _____ you _____ (*join*) us then?

9. When _____ I _____ (*see*) you again?

10. The children _____ (*not forgive*) you for leaving so soon.

11. The books _____ (*arrive*) by train at seven this evening. _____ you _____ (*go*) to the station to collect them?

12. Where _____ they _____ (*spend*) their honeymoon? I don't think they _____ (*let*) us know.

13. The procession _____ (*start*) from the temple. It _____ (*not pass*) along Ring Road, but traffic _____ (*have*) to stop at the intersection.

PART 9

請將下列未來簡單式的句子改成用 "be going to" 的寫法來表達。

1. We will cook dinner tonight.

    → _____

2. I won't sit for the piano examination this year.

    → _____

3. He will get you a ticket for the concert.

    → _____

4. Your uncle will certainly give you a good birthday present.

    → _____

5. The whole family will shift to the new house next month.

    → _____

6. She will attend the wedding lunch on his behalf.

    → _____

7. The mayor will deliver the speech.

    → _____

8. They will leave for Greensville in a few days. They will not return to Fairtown for his wedding.

    → _____

9. I won't encourage him to eat cakes or candy. They spoil his appetite.

→ _____

10. Are you ready? We won't wait for you any longer.

→ _____

11. I'll play tennis with her this evening. Will you be the referee?

→ _____

12. Will you fetch your shoes from the cobbler this afternoon?

→ _____

13. Will we have a swim before we go back to the chalet?

→ _____

14. It won't rain. The wind will blow those dark clouds away.

→ _____

PART 10

請根據提示在空格中填入正確的未來簡單式動詞（限用 will）。

1. She _____ (*travel*) by train; she told us yesterday.

2. No one _____ (*listen*) to you next time if you don't keep your promise now.

3. It _____ (*rain*) any minute now. _____ you please _____ (*bring*) your umbrella?

4. He _____ (*drive*) the car to work.

5. I _____ (*not do*) any more favors for you.

6. The birds _____ (*fly*) away as soon as you go near them.

7. Whom _____ you _____ (*invite*) to your wedding, Alice?

8. The film _____ probably _____ (*end*) at five o'clock. Halfway through it, there _____ (*be*) an intermission of ten minutes.

9. How _____ you _____ (*tell*) her that we broke her camera?

10. Do you think his parents _____ (*allow*) him to go camping with us?

11. I think I _____ (*take*) some medicine. I have been sneezing all morning.

12. When the festival is over, all of us _____ (*go*) to the seaside for a holiday.

13. Mrs. Hanson _____ (*demonstrate*) how to cook certain European dishes at the Women's Club tomorrow.

PART 11

請根據提示在空格中填入正確的未來簡單式動詞（限用 will 或 shall）。

1. The rain is beating in. I _____ (*shut*) the windows. I think it _____ (*rain*) the whole night through.

2. She _____ (*help*) me make the chicken soup. She promised me yesterday. Probably she _____ (*come*) in the afternoon.

3. I certainly must go now. I _____ (*come*) again as soon as I can.

4. Many of them _____ (*not believe*) your words, but you _____ (*convince*) them with your persuasive powers.

5. When he comes, I _____ (*ask*) him when he _____ (*take*) them to the circus.

6. We _____ (*know*) the results of the contest in a few minutes. We _____ (*not leave*) now.

7. I'm sure you _____ (*need*) a can opener. _____ I _____ (*get*) one for you?

8. _____ you _____ (*throw*) away all these books? If you sell them, they _____ (*fetch*) at least a few dollars.

9. Look! The helicopter _____ (*land*) on the field. _____ we _____ (*go*) to have a closer look?

10. There's no point in pleading with them. They _____ (*not open*) the gate for us.

11. You'd better hurry up. The train _____ (*leave*) any minute now.

12. When _____ your father _____ (*come*) back? We _____ (*not wait*) for him if he comes home late.

13. What _____ you _____ (*do*) when you grow up? _____ you _____ (*be*) a doctor like your father?

14. Don't give him so much money. He _____ (*spend*) it all within a short time. He _____ (*not set*) aside any for later use.

15. I _____ (*see*) the manager himself. He _____ (*tell*) me the reason for discharging me.

PART 12

請根據提示在空格中填入正確的現在進行式動詞。

1. Do you know who _____ (*make*) so much noise?

2. It _____ (*get*) more and more dangerous every minute.

3. All of us _____ (*go*) to the movies tonight. _____ you _____ (*come*) with us?

4. He _____ always _____ (*make*) fun of all the other boys.

5. The school bell _____ (*ring*). All the children _____ (*line*) up on the field.

6. "Where _____ you _____ (*go*) at this hour?" "Oh, I _____ (*go*) out for a breath of fresh air."

7. Many people _____ (*suffer*), but nothing _____ (*do*) to help relieve their pain.

8. Look! The water _____ (*boil*). _____ you _____ (*not go*) to turn off the cooker?

9. Karen _____ (*make*) some jam tarts. She _____ (*prepare*) for her birthday party which she _____ (*give*) for her friends.

10. Look! Do you see Allen over there? He _____ (*walk*) toward the bus stop. Now, he _____ (*turn*) and _____ (*look*) in our direction. He has seen us and _____ (*wave*) to us.

PART 13

請根據提示在空格中填入正確的現在進行式動詞。

1. We _____ (*have*) tea now. She _____ (*boil*) the water for it.

2. The disease _____ (*spread*) gradually. The health authorities _____ (*take*) measures to stop it.

3. Everybody _____ (*look*) forward to the Super Bowl to be held at the stadium next week.

4. Your taxi _____ (*wait*) for you outside. _____ everyone _____ (*go*) to the railway station with you?

5. One of these flowers _____ (*droop*), but the others _____ (*look*) fine.

6. The crops _____ (*grow*) well. The farmers _____ (*expect*) a bumper

harvest this year.

7. Mary _____ (*bake*) some cakes for the party tomorrow. She _____ (*sift*) some flour now.

8. What _____ he _____ (*laugh*) at? _____ he _____ (*not do*) his work?

9. Helen _____ (*use*) the scissors now. She _____ (*cut*) some material for a dress.

10. One worker _____ (*grease*) part of the machine while another _____ (*check*) the engine.

11. My brother _____ (*clean*) the aquarium while my sister _____ (*water*) the plants in the garden.

12. My friend and his family _____ (*move*) to a new house next week. I _____ (*help*) them to shift their furniture.

13. My mother _____ (*cook*) dinner and _____ (*listen*) to the radio at the same time.

14. His father _____ (*work*) late tonight. A colleague _____ (*take*) him home after he finishes his work.

15. I _____ (*not expect*) my friend to come, but I _____ (*wonder*) whether he will come or not.

16. The coach _____ (*select*) players for the team. Kevin _____ (*hope*) that he will be chosen.

PART 14

請根據提示在空格中填入合適的現在簡單式或現在進行式動詞。

1. He _____ (*shut*) the door as he _____ (*want*) to record his voice on the tape recorder. No one _____ (*be*) to disturb him.

2. They _____ (*like*) to read books by Jane Austen. They _____ (*read*) *Northanger Abbey* now.

3. I usually _____ (*not wear*) a coat, but I _____ (*wear*) one now because the room _____ (*be*) very cold.

4. She often _____ (*interfere*) while we _____ (*do*) the housework.

5. They _____ (attend) the buffet party at David's house tonight. The party _____ (start) at eight o'clock.

6. _____ (Be) you unhappy with the results of the examination? Everyone _____ (congratulate) you on your success. They _____ (expect) a treat from you.

7. He _____ (drive) to work every morning, but today he _____ (take) the bus. His car _____ (be) in the garage for an overhaul.

8. Someone _____ (knock) at the door. Andy _____ (walk) to the door to open it. It _____ (be) his friend Michael. They _____ (go) to the scouts' meeting together.

9. She always _____ (talk) a lot, but tonight she _____ (not talk) much as she _____ (suffer) from mouth ulcers. She _____ (be) not only silent, but she _____ (not eat) at all.

PART 15

請根據提示在空格中填入合適的現在簡單式或現在進行式動詞。

1. The new department store _____ (open) on the first day of next month.

2. It _____ (get) dark, but she _____ (not want) to go home yet. She _____ (say) that she _____ (not have) anything to do at home.

3. Every morning, she _____ (do) the cooking while we _____ (dress) for school.

4. Here _____ (come) Mr. Brown. He _____ (help) us to draw the lines for our badminton court.

5. I _____ (speak) from a telephone booth in town. Please _____ (come) to fetch me home. It _____ (rain) hard.

6. I _____ (have) a cold today. That is why I _____ (stay) at home instead of going to school.

7. _____ he _____ (come) with us? Please _____ (tell) him to hurry up. We _____ (not have) much time left.

8. We _____ (have) our lunch at that restaurant every day. It _____ (sell) roast chicken which _____ (be) the most delicious in town. We _____

(*take*) our friend, Nelson, there today.

9. This book _____ (*consist*) of three volumes. Now, _____ you
_____ (*understand*) why I _____ (*take*) such a long time to read it?

10. He _____ (*be*) a retired army officer and _____ (*like*) to tell everyone
about his adventures in the last war. The children _____ (*listen*) to him now.
_____ they _____ (*understand*) what he tells them?

11. They _____ (*not like*) to eat mangoes; that is why they _____ (*give*)
them away.

PART 16

請根據提示在空格中填入合適的現在簡單式或現在進行式動詞。

1. I _____ (*go*) to the movies tonight. I _____ (*think*) he
_____ (*want*) to go, too.

2. Something _____ (*burn*). I _____ (*wonder*) what it _____
(*be*).

3. The beggar _____ (be) blind. He _____ (*feel*) his way about with his
stick.

4. She _____ (*wait*) outside for you. She _____ (*say*) that she
_____ (*want*) to talk to you.

5. I _____ (*leave*) for America on Saturday. The ship _____ (*leave*) the
port at 5 p.m.

6. "Why _____ you _____ (*shiver*)? _____ you
_____ (*feel*) cold?" "Yes, I _____ (*be*) cold."

7. They _____ (*discuss*) a very important matter. Alice _____ (*think*)
that it _____ (*have*) something to do with the theft.

8. John and Peter _____ (*have*) a long conversation. _____ you
_____ (*know*) what they _____ (*talk*) about?

9. The manager _____ (*not like*) Mrs. Brown at all. That _____ (*be*) why
he _____ (*not leave*) the business to her.

10. She _____ (*be*) young, but she _____ (*be*) intelligent and
_____ (*understand*) everything he _____ (*say*).

基礎文法寶典 ❸
Essential English Usage & Grammar

11. She _____ (*have*) a cold. That _____ (*be*) why she _____

(*need*) to lie down. The doctor _____ (*come*) to see her later in the day.

12. I _____ (*wonder*) why the dog _____ (*bark*). Oh, I _____

(*hear*) footsteps now. Someone _____ (*come*) up the path to the front door.

13. "_____ this bag _____ (*belong*) to you?" "No, it _____

(*do not*). It _____ (*belong*) to Mary. She _____ (*bring*) her books in

it."

14. I _____ (*try*) to listen to some music, but my brother _____ (*have*) his

bath now, and he _____ (*sing*) at the top of his voice.

15. She _____ (*lose*) her temper very often now. When she _____ (*do*) so,

she _____ (*scream*) all the time. Listen! _____ you

_____ (*hear*) her? She _____ (*yell*) at her brother now.

PART 17

請根據提示在空格中填入合適的現在簡單式或現在進行式動詞。

1. The team of football players _____ (*be*) very strong. They _____

(*practice*) whenever they _____ (*have*) the time. Right now, they

_____ (*play*) in the field even though it _____ (*rain*).

2. The movie theater _____ (*show*) this film now. If your friend _____

(*want*) to see it with us, _____ (*tell*) her that we will meet her at the movie theater

half an hour before the film _____ (*start*).

3. The sky _____ (*be*) dark and cloudy; a strong wind _____ (*blow*). The

trees _____ (*sway*) and the birds _____ (*fly*) to their nests. I

_____ (*think*) there is going to be a heavy shower.

4. The party _____ (*be*) a great success. Not a single person _____ (*sit*)

down; everyone _____ (*dance*) and _____ (*enjoy*) himself.

5. I _____ (*have*) a sewing box which _____ (*contain*) all the things I

_____ (*need*). I _____ (*sew*) a shirt for my brother; I

_____ (*hope*) he _____ (*like*) it.

6. If you _____ (*go*) to town now, I _____ (*want*) you to buy some green

thread for me. I _____ (*make*) a green dress and I _____ (*need*) the thread. If there _____ (*be not*) any green thread, _____ (*buy*) a reel of white thread instead.

7. Arthur _____ (*like*) to read. Whenever he _____ (*be*) free, he _____ (*take*) out a book and _____ (*read*) it quietly. Now he _____ (*study*) the dictionary.

8. We _____ (*stage*) our concert next week. We _____ (*do*) everything to make it a success, for the parents of students and important guests _____ (*come*).

9. It _____ (*be*) nine at night now. I _____ (*go*) to the station to send my sister off. She _____ (*travel*) on the night train. _____ you _____ (*come*) with me?

10. Everywhere boys _____ (*fly*) their kites. They either _____ (*buy*) them at shops or _____ (*make*) their own.

11. Every morning she _____ (*sweep*) the floor and _____ (*dust*) the tables. She always _____ (*grumble*) about the amount of work she _____ (*have*) to do.

12. There _____ (*be*) lots of flowers in my garden. My father _____ (*take*) care of them. He often _____ (*exchange*) plants with his friends. Now, he _____ (*plant*) a fern which he _____ (*say*) is very rare.

13. I _____ (*have*) a lot of work to do, so I _____ (*not go*) to town tonight. Besides, I _____ (*feel*) rather tired and I _____ (*want*) to go to bed early.

14. If your sister _____ (*come*) home and _____ (*ask*) you where I _____ (*be*), tell her I _____ (*wait*) for her at my place. I _____ (*have*) a surprise for her and I _____ (*hope*) she _____ (*like*) it.

15. As I _____ (*walk*) along the shore, I _____ (*gaze*) at the sea. I _____ (*hear*) the sound of waves which _____ (*break*) gently against the rocks. On the beach, crabs _____ (*crawl*) from their tiny holes; boys with sticks _____ (*try*) to dig them out.

16. Every afternoon I _____ (*take*) a bath, but I can't this afternoon. My brother

_____ (*repaint*) the bathroom and I have to wait till the paint _____ (*dry*).

17. You cannot enter the library now. The librarians _____ (*clean*) the library. They _____ (*take*) down the books and _____ (*dust*) the shelves.

18. The circus _____ (*come*)! Children _____ (*run*) out to the roadside, _____ (*shout*) and _____ (*wave*) to the circus performers. Mothers _____ (*have*) a hard time controlling the children.

19. The sky _____ (*be*) dark but the fishermen _____ (*put*) their boats out to sea. On the beach, their wives _____ (*watch*) anxiously. Some _____ (*try*) to persuade the men not to go.

PART 18

請根據提示在空格中填入合適的現在簡單式或現在進行式動詞。

1. Mr. Lea and Mr. Brown _____ (*have*) a long conversation. I _____ (*wonder*) what they _____ (*talk*) about.

2. The committee _____ (*discuss*) some important issues. They _____ (*have*) another meeting tomorrow.

3. He never _____ (*listen*) to a word that his mother _____ (*say*). He _____ always _____ (*think*) about something else.

4. We _____ (*organize*) a trip to Pirates' Cove, but he cannot come with us as he _____ (*have*) a high fever.

5. He often _____ (*travel*) to Skyline Bay by train and while he _____ (*travel*), he _____ (*enjoy*) reading a book. Sometimes when he _____ (*feel*) tired, he _____ (*sleep*) during the journey.

6. In his letter, my brother _____ (*say*) that he _____ (*come*) home next Monday. He _____ (*sail*) on the liner "Sea Maiden," which _____ (*make*) regular trips between Okinawa and Keelung.

7. I _____ (*write*) to Mary, and I _____ (*want*) to tell her that we _____ (*miss*) her very much.

8. "Please _____ (*go*) to see if the rain _____ (*come*) into the room. If it _____ (*be*), please _____ (*shut*) the windows," my mother said.

9. _____ you _____ (*see*) the monkey that _____ (*climb*) up

the coconut tree? When it _____ (*reach*) the top of the tree, it _____

(*pick*) the coconuts and _____ (*drop*) them down.

10. The telephone _____ (*ring*), but no one _____ (*answer*) it because

everyone _____ (*be*) in the garden.

11. He _____ (*make*) some appreciative noises as he _____ (*taste*) the

soup. My mother _____ (*look*) very pleased.

12. He _____ (*hate*) to be disturbed while he _____ (*have*) a meal. Even

when his friends _____ (*call*) on him, he _____ (*refuse*) to leave the

table until he has finished.

13. Old Mrs. Jones always _____ (*grumble*) about the weather, whether it

_____ (*rain*) or whether the sun _____ (*shine*). Apart from this, she

_____ (*seem*) to be a very kind person.

14. "What _____ you _____ (*wait*) for? The shops _____ (*be*)

not open yet," he said. "I _____ (*know*) that, but I _____ (*want*) to be

early because they _____ (*have*) a big sale today."

PART 19

請根據提示在空格中填入合適的現在簡單式或現在進行式動詞。

1. They _____ (*work*) late tonight. There _____ (*be*) a lot of work to be

done.

2. The rooster _____ (*crow*). I _____ (*think*) it _____ (*be*)

morning now.

3. Look! Some birds _____ (*fly*) down. They _____ (*eat*) the

breadcrumbs I left outside.

4. We _____ (*go*) to the beach this weekend. We _____ (*hope*) the

weather will be fine.

5. It _____ (*rain*) quite heavily. I _____ (*believe*) it will keep up.

6. His wife _____ always _____ (*nag*) at him. I _____

(*think*) he has grown used to it now. He _____ (*not seem*) to hear her at all!

7. My mother usually _____ (*feed*) the chickens, but I _____ (*do*) so

now because she _____ (*have*) a lot of other work to do.

8. The cat _____ (*lie*) under the table. It _____ (*sleep*).

9. It _____ (*not matter*). They usually _____ (*bring*) extra food.

10. It _____ (*get*) darker. The sun _____ (*disappear*) behind the mountains.

11. All of us _____ (*go*) on a picnic tomorrow except Henry, who _____ (*stay*) at home because he _____ (*have*) a slight fever.

12. Charles _____ (*boast*) a lot. He _____ always _____ (*tell*) us about his achievements.

13. My sister _____ (*have*) her bath. She _____ (*sing*) in the bathroom.

14. The dog _____ (*recognize*) its old friend. It _____ (*bark*) joyfully and _____ (*wag*) its tail.

15. _____ you _____ (*understand*) what that lady _____ (*say*) now? She _____ (*seem*) to be talking in some strange language.

16. _____ they _____ (*have*) a meeting in the room? What _____ they _____ (*discuss*)?

17. The water _____ (*contain*) too much chlorine. _____ you _____ (*smell*) it?

18. My mother _____ (*know*) their family very well. They _____ always _____ (*come*) to visit us.

19. Jimmy _____ (*not want*) to come with us. He _____ (*prefer*) to stay at home. He _____ (*watch*) television now.

20. He _____ always _____ (*talk*) to me as though I were a child. I _____ (*wish*) he would realize I _____ (*be*) twenty years old now.

PART 20

請根據提示在空格中填入正確的過去進行式動詞。

1. We _____ (*talk*) when the teacher came in.

2. While we _____ (*stand*) there, they _____ (*chat*) away as if we didn't exist.

3. The baby _____ (*cry*) while his mother _____ (*prepare*) his milk.

4. She _____ always _____ (*sew*) when I visited her.

5. He _____ (*finish*) his composition while I _____ just _____ (*begin*).

6. They _____ always _____ (*complain*) about the leaking roof, but they would do nothing about it.

7. She _____ still _____ (*work*) after all the others had gone to bed.

8. While they _____ (*swim*), he _____ (*sunbathe*) on the beach.

9. My father _____ (*water*) the plants while my mother _____ (*cook*) in the kitchen.

10. The students _____ (*not listen*) while the teacher _____ (*talk*).

11. I _____ (*read*) in the library while the rest _____ (*do*) experiments in the laboratory.

12. When I _____ (*pass*) by her house, I saw her at the gate.

13. The boys _____ (*set*) up the tents while the girls _____ (*cook*).

14. The thieves _____ (*run*) away when the policemen arrived.

15. Susan _____ (*search*) for the purse that she had lost and _____ (*grumble*) at the same time.

16. The dogs _____ (*bark*) at the old man who _____ (*limp*) down the lane.

PART 21

請根據提示在空格中填入正確的過去進行式動詞。

1. He _____ (*wear*) a pair of dark glasses when I saw him.

2. His room was in a mess as he _____ (*redecorate*) it.

3. Although there was no one in the car, the engine _____ (*run*).

4. The two boys _____ (*shout*) and _____ (*fight*) while a passer-by _____ (*try*) to pull them apart.

5. I _____ (*have*) tea while she _____ (*sew*) a dress.

6. While he _____ (*learn*) how to ride a bicycle, he had a few accidents.

7. We _____ (*collect*) wood for the campfire when we saw a snake.

8. The fire _____ still _____ (*burn*) this morning.

9. The red ants _____ (*crawl*) all over his body and he _____ (*try*) to shake them off.

10. She _____ (*prepare*) dinner while he _____ (*mow*) the lawn.

11. He said that he _____ (*walk*) here when he saw the accident.

12. She _____ always _____ (*find*) fault with people; nothing could ever please her.

13. I _____ still _____ (*hope*) that he would agree to go with us.

14. Everyone _____ (*listen*) as he _____ (*read*) the letter.

15. "What _____ you _____ (*do*) last night? _____ you _____ (*practice*)?" "No, I wasn't. I _____ (*study*).

PART 22

請根據提示在空格中填入合適的過去簡單式或過去進行式動詞。

1. She _____ (*get*) into the car when she _____ (*realize*) that she had forgotten to lock up the house.

2. I _____ (*hold*) an umbrella, but the wind _____ (*be*) so strong that it _____ (*blow*) it inside out.

3. I _____ (*know*) something odd _____ (*happen*), so I _____ (*go*) in to investigate.

4. He _____ (*hide*) behind some boxes while we _____ (*search*) for him in the bedroom.

5. I _____ (*stand*) outside, so he _____ (*invite*) me in and _____ (*bring*) a chair for me.

6. As we _____ (*walk*) home after school, it _____ (*begin*) to rain heavily, so we _____ (*run*) into a nearby shop for shelter.

7. The teacher _____ (*explain*) the method when Janet _____ (*stand*) up and _____ (*ask*) him a question.

8. It _____ (*rain*) heavily, so we _____ (*sit*) around the fire to warm ourselves.

9. A fiery spark _____ (*fall*) on my shirt. Before we _____ (*know*) what _____ (*happen*), the shirt _____ (*be*) on fire.

10. Although I _____ (arrive) half an hour late, they _____ still _____ (stand) on the pavement, waiting for me.

11. They _____ always _____ (grumble) about the work, but actually they _____ (be) more contented than they _____ (realize).

12. I _____ (think) that the problem _____ (be) very easy, but when I _____ (try) to solve it, I _____ (find) out how difficult it really _____ (be).

13. The child _____ (sleep) in his room when the fire _____ (break) out. Luckily, the firemen _____ (be) able to enter the house and _____ (rescue) him.

14. Nancy _____ (wait) outside the garage while her father _____ (get) the car started. When the car engine _____ (run), she _____ (get) into the car, and both of them _____ (drive) off.

PART 23

請根據提示在空格中填入合適的過去簡單式或過去進行式動詞。

1. The man _____ (clean) his pistol when it accidentally _____ (go) off and _____ (kill) him.

2. The traffic policeman _____ (stop) him because he _____ (speed).

3. When I _____ (come) in, Karen _____ (discuss) a problem with a friend. She _____ (break) off that discussion and _____ (invite) me to sit down.

4. While the band _____ (play), many people _____ (dance) but there were also some who _____ (dine).

5. The man _____ (spend) every cent that he _____ (have) because he _____ (know) he was going to die soon.

6. I _____ (search) for my friend when I _____ (see) him among a crowd of girls. He _____ (talk) to them and _____ (wave) his arms about.

7. The burglar _____ (open) the door of the safe when he _____ (hear) footsteps. He _____ (pause) and _____ (listen) to find out if the

sounds _____ (*come*) any nearer.

8. As I _____ (*drive*) along the coast road, I _____ (*notice*) many yachts out at sea. They _____ (*sail*) toward the bay.

9. When I _____ (*arrive*) at the movie theater, Richard _____ (*wait*) for me.

10. My friend _____ always _____ (*complain*) about her flat. She _____ (*say*) she _____ (*not like*) it and _____ (*try*) to find another.

11. I _____ (*walk*) across the field while a soccer game was in progress. I _____ (*not know*) the ball _____ (*come*) in my direction until it _____ (*hit*) me.

12. While I _____ (*stay*) with my uncle in Greenwood Park, I often _____ (*accompany*) him on his fishing trips.

13. As we _____ (*drive*) along the Federal Highway, a policeman _____ (*stop*) us. He _____ (*tell*) us that he _____ (*look*) for stolen goods and _____ (*order*) us out of our car.

14. He _____ (*dress*) when his friend _____ (*call*) him. As he _____ (*rush*) down the stairs, he _____ (*trip*) over a toy and _____ (*fall*).

15. It _____ (*rain*) while we _____ (*wait*) for the bus. Lightning _____ (*streak*) across the sky and thunder _____ (*rumble*).

PART 24

請根據提示在空格中填入合適的過去簡單式或過去進行式動詞。

1. When I _____ (*enter*) the room, he _____ (*talk*) to someone on the telephone.

2. She _____ (*cook*) dinner when the fire _____ (*start*) in the kitchen.

3. The little girl _____ (*fall*) down when she _____ (*run*) home. She _____ still _____ (*cry*) when she _____ (*reach*) home.

4. While they _____ (*fight*) over the money, he quietly _____ (*escape*).

5. While all of us _____ (*look*) for him, he _____ (*sleep*) peacefully in

his room.

6. As Tom _____ (*walk*) down the road, he _____ (*step*) on a banana

peel and _____ (*fall*) heavily.

7. He _____ (*carry*) an open umbrella as it _____ (*rain*) quite heavily.

When he _____ (*see*) the bus coming, he quickly _____ (*shut*) the

umbrella and _____ (*run*) toward the bus.

8. He _____ (*read*) an exciting story when the lights _____ (*go*) out.

They _____ (*not come*) on till three hours later.

9. Why _____ you _____ (*interrupt*) us just now? We _____

(*have*) an interesting discussion on politics.

10. She _____ (*seem*) quite happy when I _____ (*see*) her this morning.

11. As they _____ (*search*) for the key, they _____ (*find*) an unopened

letter addressed to him.

12. The postman _____ (*cycle*) down the road when the dogs in the neighborhood

_____ (*start*) to chase him.

13. Susan _____ (*have*) her bath when the telephone _____ (*ring*). Her

mother _____ (*cook*) in the kitchen and _____ (*have*) no time to

answer it.

14. He _____ (*water*) the plants in the garden when a bee _____ (*sting*)

him on the hand. His hand _____ (*swell*) up almost at once.

15. The members of the club _____ still _____ (*argue*) about the matter

when the chairman _____ (*arrive*).

16. He _____ (*drive*) down the road when a policeman _____ (*stop*) his

car and _____ (*ask*) to see his license.

17. I _____ (*listen*) to the news on the radio when I _____ (*hear*) a knock

on the door. I _____ (*open*) it and _____ (*see*) a small boy standing on

the doorstep.

PART 25

請根據提示在空格中填入合適的過去簡單式或過去進行式動詞。

1. I _____ (*take*) a stroll along the beach when I _____ (*hear*) a cry for

help. There _____ (*be*) a little boy in the water. I _____ (*run*) into the water and _____ (*bring*) him to safety.

2. He _____ still _____ (*read*) the book when I _____ (*go*) to borrow it from him.

3. Jenny _____ (*paint*) the living room when she _____ (*knock*) over the pot of paint.

4. She _____ (*remind*) us about the date for handing in our compositions, but we _____ (*not listen*) to her.

5. Mrs. Jones suddenly _____ (*wake*) her husband up and _____ (*tell*) him that someone _____ (*try*) to break into the house.

6. When we last _____ (*see*) Tommy, he _____ (*hurry*) toward the railway station.

7. I _____ (*wave*) to him while I _____ (*be*) on the bus yesterday. I wonder if he _____ (*see*) me.

8. We _____ (*not recognize*) him till he _____ (*start*) talking to us.

9. The traffic lights _____ (*not work*) and my father _____ (*not know*) whether to stop the car or not.

10. She _____ (*carry*) the pot of tea into the living room when she _____ (*slip*) on the rug.

11. We _____ (*write*) to each other until he suddenly _____ (*stop*) replying to my letters.

12. His bag _____ still _____ (*lie*) where he had left it. He _____ (*open*) it quickly to see if anything _____ (*be*) missing.

13. They _____ (*eat*) peanuts when I _____ (*go*) into the garden. They _____ (*offer*) some to me but I _____ (*not take*) any.

PART 26

請根據提示在空格中填入合適的過去簡單式或過去進行式動詞。

1. It _____ (*rain*) quite heavily by the time we _____ (*reach*) home.

2. She _____ (*start*) to cry as they _____ (*get*) into the car.

3. When I _____ (*reach*) the house, I _____ (*find*) them quarreling.

4. I _____ (*study*) in my room when the telephone _____ (*ring*).

5. All of them _____ (*discuss*) the problem when Edward _____ (*come*) rushing into the room.

6. They _____ (*shout*) at each other when I _____ (*leave*) the house.

7. He _____ (*take*) your wallet while you _____ (*not look*).

8. As we _____ (*go*) around the bend, the car _____ (*skid*) off the road and _____ (*land*) in the ditch.

9. As he _____ (*write*) a letter, he _____ (*hear*) a knock at the door. When he _____ (*open*) the door, he _____ (*find*) nobody there.

10. When I _____ (*see*) him, he _____ (*trim*) the garden hedge. Just then, as I _____ (*talk*) to him, he _____ (*cut*) himself.

11. While he _____ (*carry*) a heavy box, he _____ (*trip*) and _____ (*fall*) down. I _____ (*run*) to help him, but he _____ (*manage*) to get up by himself.

12. As I _____ (*press*) the bell, I _____ (*hear*) some strange noises which _____ (*come*) from inside the house.

13. When I _____ (*go*) to her house, she _____ (*prepare*) dinner. I _____ (*ask*) her if she would help me with my homework. She _____ (*agree*) to do so after preparing the meal.

PART 27

請根據提示在空格中填入正確的未來進行式動詞。

1. When _____ you _____ (*have*) your next singing lesson?

2. They _____ (*not come*) here again! I forbid you to invite them.

3. The postman _____ (*pass*) by soon. You can ask him to mail the letter for you.

4. They _____ (*spend*) the night at their cousin's house as it will be too late for them to come back.

5. The sky is so dark. It _____ probably _____ (*rain*) by the time that we reach the seaside.

6. My eldest brother _____ (*come*) back next month. You must meet him.

7. The professor _____ (*lecture*) at eight o'clock instead of at nine.

8. We _____ (*not sail*) this afternoon. The sea is too rough.

9. My father _____ (*drive*) us to school all week because we have not found a taxi to take us yet.

10. "Mother told me that she _____ (*not make*) any cakes this Sunday. She _____ (*attend*) a club meeting," I said to my sister.

11. The tourists _____ (*not stay*) long on Paradise Island as they have only a limited time to tour the Far East.

12. The Dramatic Society _____ (*put*) on another play soon. _____ you _____ (*participate*) in it again?

13. When we go to visit her, she _____ probably _____ (*weed*) the garden.

14. Please don't come in the afternoon, Mr. Parker, for my father _____ (*have*) a nap.

15. The interviewers _____ (*observe*) your every movement the moment you enter the room.

16. We still have plenty of time to go around the village for the bus _____ (*not leave*) until half past three.

17. Many people _____ (*listen*) to you and _____ (*watch*) you when you appear on television.

18. Mr. Harper, the history teacher, _____ (*teach*) us next year, and we _____ (*take*) down notes for every lesson.

19. Next year, more students _____ (*leave*) school, and the majority of them _____ (*look*) for jobs.

20. My sister _____ (*sleep*) by the time that I return, but my parents _____ (*wait*) up for me.

PART 28

請根據提示在空格中填入正確的未來進行式動詞。

1. When you arrive, I _____ probably _____ (*cook*) in the kitchen, so don't hesitate to come right in.

2. My sister _____ (*take*) part in the school debate again this year. She won a prize last year.

3. We _____ (*travel*) to the coast while you are still in bed.

4. By the time she discovers the loss, they _____ (*fly*) thousands of kilometers away.

5. It _____ (*rain*) by the time we reach the zoo. There's no point in walking around the zoo in the rain, is there?

6. Ricky _____ (*come*) to visit us this Sunday. You can talk to him then.

7. What _____ you _____ (*do*) tomorrow? _____ you _____ (*work*) in the garden as usual?

8. We _____ (*go*) your way. We can give you a ride if you like.

9. They _____ (*look*) for us if we don't return by noon.

10. The train _____ (*arrive*) at 2 a.m. tomorrow morning. All of you _____ (*sleep*) then.

11. My mother _____ (*work*) in the kitchen at this hour and my father _____ (*have*) his nap.

12. I can't attend the parade, but I _____ (*watch*) it on television.

13. When he takes his walk, we _____ (*wait*) at the corner.

14. "The injury to his foot is not all that bad. He _____ (*walk*) again in a week," the doctor said.

15. The airplane _____ (*take*) off in a few minutes. The flight attendant _____ (*tell*) us to fasten our seat belts soon.

16. When they come back, the dog _____ (*wait*) for them at the gate. It _____ (*wag*) its tail and _____ (*bark*) away, too.

17. At six o'clock tomorrow, the tide _____ (*come*) in. We _____ (*sail*) off with the tide.

18. Where _____ you _____ (*live*) twenty years from now? Perhaps people _____ (*have*) homes on the Moon.

PART 29

請根據提示在空格中填入正確的未來進行式動詞。

1. I _____ (*sweep*) the garden while you boys are cleaning out the garage.

2. He _____ (*visit*) me soon, so I'll tell him the news then.

3. You _____ (*sit*) for your examinations next week. Are you well-prepared?

4. We _____ (*work*) late tonight, so you had better not wait for us.

5. My cousin _____ (*leave*) at the end of the month; you will still be able to see her before she goes.

6. Don't you think we should rest for a while? Otherwise, we _____ (*gasp*) for breath by the time we reach the top of the hill.

7. Don't say anything foolish when you go in. They _____ (*watch*) you to find fault with you.

8. _____ he _____ (*bring*) any friends along when he comes down for the holidays next week?

9. If we plant the seeds now, the flowers _____ (*bloom*) by the time Mother comes home from the hospital.

10. Get ready as quickly as you can. The taxi _____ (*come*) here in five minutes.

11. When they come, you must entertain them. I _____ (*prepare*) dinner in the kitchen.

12. I don't think it _____ still _____ (*rain*) when it is time for us to go out.

13. "I _____ (*clean*) the stove while you are chopping the firewood." "All right, but what _____ John _____ (*do*)?" "Oh, he _____ (*catch*) some fish for supper."

PART 30

請根據提示在空格中填入合適的未來簡單式或未來進行式動詞。

1. Notice on the board: All students _____ (*assemble*) in the hall every Friday morning.

2. At this time tomorrow he _____ (*fly*) to Sydney.

3. I hope that you _____ (*do*) well in the examination. I _____ (*pray*) for you.

4. _____ you please _____ (*put*) the typewriter here?

5. The bus drivers are on strike. We _____ (*walk*) to school tomorrow.

6. Don't worry about us. We _____ (*take*) good care of ourselves.

7. Aren't you ready yet? The show _____ (*start*) in a few minutes.

8. I don't like that boy and I _____ (*not help*) him with his work.

9. Alex _____ (*not come*) to school for a week because he is down with mumps.

10. He _____ (*not act*) in the play because he has a sore throat. We _____ (*have*) to find someone to replace him.

11. She is feeling cold. She _____ (*not open*) the windows.

12. The Government _____ (*pull*) down all the old houses along this road in a few years.

13. We _____ (*wait*) for you outside. _____ you _____ (*finish*) your work quickly and come out?

14. In a few days, they _____ (*celebrate*) Christmas. Every Christian family _____ (*buy*) presents and many _____ (*decorate*) Christmas trees.

15. Why did you hide his shoes? He _____ (*look*) for them everywhere tomorrow.

16. Mr. Hunter _____ (*not be*) at home tonight. He _____ (*attend*) a dinner at the hotel.

17. I'm not feeling well. I don't think that I _____ (*play*) table tennis with you this evening. _____ you _____ (*ask*) someone to take my place?

18. I _____ (*see*) Winnie at the library this evening. I can give her your message then.

PART 31

請根據提示在空格中填入正確的現在完成式動詞，並將副詞放在正確的位置。

1. We _____ (*just have*) a basketball game with our English teacher.

2. They _____ (*already receive*) their orders, but they _____ (*not carry*) them out yet.

3. I _____ (*often help*) him around the garden, and he _____ (*often teach*) me how to take care of plants.

4. _____ he _____ (*ever show*) you how the experiment is carried out?

5. I _____ (*seldom speak*) to him about such things.

6. We _____ (*never be*) to Uncle Bill's house before because he lives so far away.

7. Such a thing _____ (*never happen*) before, and she does not know what to do.

8. You _____ (*spoil*) the whole evening by losing your temper. I hope you won't do so again.

9. Some of the boys _____ (*just decide*) to throw a party in celebration of the end of the school term.

10. Mr. Robinson _____ (*recently complete*) a book called *The Art of Interior Decoration* and it will be published soon.

11. _____ she _____ (*ever confide*) in you?

12. My mother _____ (*just make*) some tea. Do stay for a cup.

13. It _____ (*almost take*) every ounce of his energy to move the boulder off the road.

14. We _____ (*nearly finish*) cleaning the room; we _____ (*just mop*) the floor, so please don't come in yet.

15. The girls _____ (*never be*) late for a meeting before. I think they _____ (*completely forget*) about it.

16. I _____ (*just hear*) the news that the school examination is going to be postponed. _____ you _____ (*hear*) anything about it?

17. Aunt Emma _____ (*often win*) prizes for her talent in flower decoration. _____ you _____ (*ever be*) to a flower show?

18. They _____ (*always try*) to make us sell them our piece of land, but we _____ (*always refuse*) them.

PART 32

請根據提示在空格中填入正確的現在完成式動詞。

1. He _____ (*ask*) me that question several times.

2. _____ the taxi _____ (*arrive*) yet, John?

3. I think he _____ (*do*) all the work which I had given him.

4. Look! Somebody _____ (*drop*) a wallet there on the road.

5. I _____ already _____ (*tell*) her many times not to do that again.

6. _____ she _____ (*sweep*) the house and the garden path yet?

7. I _____ (*ask*) him to let me go, but he _____ (*refuse*).

8. _____ you _____ (*think*) over this matter yet? You _____ (*take*) a long time to make up your mind.

9. He _____ almost _____ (*forget*) about it, though I _____ (*remind*) him several times.

10. I _____ (*invite*) several friends for dinner this evening. I hope you _____ (*prepare*) enough food.

11. Miss Brown _____ (*teach*) us for some years. We _____ always _____ (*like*) her very much.

12. I _____ already _____ (*pay*) the money for the things I bought, but I _____ (*not* get) my change yet.

13. He _____ already _____ (*leave*) for Long Beach, but I think the plane _____ (*not arrive*) there yet.

14. This vase _____ (*be*) in my family for many years. My mother _____ (*take*) good care of it.

15. I think Christopher _____ already _____ (*leave*). Probably he _____ (*go*) home. I _____ (*not see*) him for over an hour.

16. _____ any of you _____ (*see*) my book? I _____ (*lose*) it.

17. He _____ just _____ (*return*) from New Island. I hope he _____ (*bring*) us presents. He _____ always _____ (*have*) a great affection for us.

18. _____ Peter _____ (*tell*) you about the meeting tonight?

PART 33

請根據提示在空格中填入正確的現在完成式動詞。

1. I _____ just _____ (*borrow*) this book from the library. _____ you _____ (*read*) it before?

2. I _____ (*buy*) the tickets, but I can't go to the movies until I _____ (*finish*) my work.

3. Everybody else _____ (*hear*) the news. _____ you _____ (*hear*) it, too?

4. The doctor _____ (*treat*) the wound and _____ (*assure*) her that she will be all right.

5. The nurse _____ (*work*) in the village hospital for many years. She _____ (*become*) very popular with the people living in the village.

6. My brother _____ (*use*) this razor before but it is still very sharp.

7. Susan _____ (*return*) from school. She _____ just _____

(*eat*) her lunch.

8. They _____ (*feed*) the chickens, but they _____ (*not feed*) the cat.

They _____ (*not prepare*) its food.

9. That is the first time that he _____ (*fight*) with the boy next door. It is unfortunate

that he _____ (*break*) his arm in the fight.

10. One must reap what one _____ (*sow*).

11. We _____ (*not make*) much progress so far. How much of the work

_____ you _____ (*do*)?

12. The bell _____ (*ring*), but the schoolchildren _____ (*not come*) out

yet.

13. He _____ finally _____ (*decide*) to go to the Greenwood Holiday

Resort for his vacation; he _____ (*not be*) there before.

14. "_____ you _____ (*think*) it over carefully? You _____

(*have*) ample time, you know," Mrs. Lea said.

15. The baby _____ (*behave*) wonderfully up to now. He _____ (*not cry*)

at all, and he _____ (*eat*) his dinner without his usual tantrum.

16. That boy _____ (*work*) very hard and _____ (*save*) up a lot of money.

PART 34

請根據提示在空格中填入正確的現在完成式動詞。

1. Mr. Biggs _____ (*leave*) a note for you. He _____ (*pin*) it to the door.

2. The machine _____ (*break*) down.

3. A little girl _____ (*fall*) into the river. A man _____ (*dive*) in to save

her.

4. _____ you _____ (*decide*) what to do? I _____ (*give*) you

sufficient time to think over my proposition.

5. We _____ (*not see*) him up to now. _____ he _____ (*be*)

to your house?

6. I _____ (*read*) for two hours but _____ (*not reach*) the center of the

book yet. I think that I _____ (*have*) enough of the book for the day.

7. Where _____ you _____ (*be*)? What _____ you _____ (*do*) to your hands? They are so dirty!

8. This pair of scissors is blunt already. I _____ (*ask*) my father to sharpen it for me.

9. He _____ (*return*) the book to her, but she _____ (*not bring*) it along.

10. It _____ (*not rain*) for a long time. The grass _____ all _____ (*dry*) up.

11. _____ Peter _____ (*write*) to you also? I _____ just _____ (*receive*) a letter from him.

12. "All my efforts _____ (*be*) in vain!" he wailed.

13. The teacher _____ already _____ (*explain*) everything to him and he _____ just _____ (*finish*) writing out his answer.

14. The boys _____ (*not go*) camping since the last holidays. They _____ just _____ (*plan*) a camping trip for next month.

15. _____ you _____ (*find*) the meanings of any of those difficult words so far?

16. They _____ (*think*) a lot about the matter and _____ finally _____ (*decide*) to cooperate with us in the project.

PART 35

請根據提示在空格中填入合適的過去簡單式或現在完成式動詞。

1. The price of butter _____ (*go*) up since last month. When I _____ (*buy*) a quarter kilogram of it last week, I _____ (*have*) to pay more for it.

2. The manager _____ already _____ (*sign*) the letter. _____ he _____ (*ask*) you to send it off for him?

3. He _____ (*not arrive*) yet. I _____ (*receive*) a letter from him three days ago saying that he would arrive today.

4. He _____ (*be*) here last week, but he _____ (*leave*) for Manchester now.

5. She _____ (*fall*) ill again. The doctor _____ already _____ (*come*) and _____ (*examine*) her.

6. The cut on his leg _____ almost _____ (*heal*). He _____

just _____ (*be*) to the clinic to change the dressing. He _____ (*hurt*)

himself when he was chopping some firewood last month.

7. _____ you ever _____ (*be*) to the Grand Canyon? I _____

(*go*) there last week and _____ (*enjoy*) the beautiful view.

8. She _____ (*ask*) us to weed her garden a week ago, but we _____ (*not*

do) it for her yet.

9. A few years ago, he _____ (*inherit*) all his father's property, but now he

_____ (*use*) it up.

10. He _____ (*teach*) her English for three years, and she _____ (*pass*)

every English examination.

11. We _____ (*wind*) the clock an hour ago, but now it _____ (*stop*).

12. He _____ just _____ (*swim*) three lengths of the pool in five minutes.

_____ you _____ (*swim*) faster than he did yesterday?

PART 36

請根據提示在空格中填入合適的過去簡單式或現在完成式動詞。

1. The detective _____ (*find*) some clues in the murder case. He _____

(*be*) here a moment ago.

2. The jelly _____ (*not set*) yet. She _____ (*not put*) it into the

refrigerator till late this afternoon.

3. She _____ (*kneel*) at the altar and _____ (*begin*) to pray.

4. " _____ you ever _____ (*ride*) a horse before?" "No, I

_____ (*not try*) doing so."

5. The postman _____ (*just be*) here. He _____ (*leave*) a parcel and a

letter.

6. We _____ (*want*) to buy those tennis balls yesterday, but we _____

(*not have*) enough money with us.

7. He _____ (*be*) very successful in his business since he _____ (*come*)

here three years ago.

8. What does a beaver look like? I _____ (*never see*) one before.

9. He _____ (*not finish*) his work yet. _____ you _____

(*watch*) him at work yesterday? _____ he _____ (*make*) any mistakes?

10. He _____ always _____ (*be*) a member of the club. He _____ (*join*) it in 1975 and _____ now _____ (*become*) its secretary.

11. He _____ (*lock*) all the windows and the doors in the house before he _____ (*drive*) to the airport.

12. Who _____ (*take*) my bag? I _____ (*leave*) it in that corner a moment ago, and now the bag _____ (*disappear*).

13. The doctor _____ (*advise*) him against eating starchy foods, but after he _____ (*leave*), his patient _____ (*go*) into the kitchen and _____ (*eat*) several of the cakes there.

PART 37

請根據提示在空格中填入合適的過去簡單式或現在完成式動詞。

1. I _____ (*not see*) Mr. Wood for three years. I _____ (*hear*) that he _____ (*go*) overseas.

2. We _____ (*email*) to the department telling them about it, and they _____ (*send*) a reply yesterday.

3. They _____ (*leave*) here about two hours ago. They _____ (*ask*) me to give this letter to you.

4. My brother _____ (*come*) home late last night. He _____ (*not get*) up yet.

5. William recently _____ (*adopt*) the habit of going for a walk every evening. I _____ (*see*) him near the park last evening.

6. The shopkeeper _____ (*deliver*) the goods you _____ (*order*) yesterday. _____ you _____ (*pay*) him yet?

7. Since she _____ (*arrive*) here last week, she _____ (*visit*) many tourist attractions.

8. He _____ (*invite*) a few friends to dinner. I hope we _____ (*prepare*) enough food for them.

9. Our father _____ (*give*) us a new puppy last week. We _____ (*name*) it "Lady."

10. "Yes, we _____ (*see*) the picture. We _____ (*see*) it when we went to town a few nights ago," he _____ (*say*).

11. She _____ (*know*) him since he was born, for they _____ (*live*) next door to each other for many years.

12. When he _____ (*find*) out everything he _____ (*want*) to know, he _____ (*start*) to plan the next course of action.

13. "_____ you _____ (*be*) to Hyde Park?" "Yes, I _____ (*be*) there a few times."

14. There _____ (*be*) a storm last evening. The rain _____ (*wash*) away the dust from the roads.

15. Someone _____ (*find*) a pen on the bench outside. _____ you _____ (*lose*) a pen while you _____ (*be*) here yesterday?

16. The nurse _____ (*give*) the patient an injection. She _____ (*take*) his temperature and pulse, too.

17. My sister _____ (*promise*) to help me with the difficult problems, but I did not need her help because I _____ (*finish*) all the sums by myself last night.

PART 38

請根據提示在空格中填入合適的過去簡單式或現在完成式動詞。

1. I _____ (*know*) him since he _____ (*be*) a child. He _____ (*change*) a great deal since then.

2. He _____ (*be*) quite pleased with my work, and he _____ (*promise*) to give me a treat next week.

3. Where _____ you _____ (*put*) it? I can't find it at all even though I _____ (*search*) everywhere for it.

4. He _____ just _____ (*finish*) his work. It _____ (*take*) him more than two hours to do it while I _____ (*do*) mine in an hour.

5. I _____ just _____ (*finish*) preparing dinner. I _____ (*start*) two hours ago, and I _____ (*make*) all your favorite dishes.

6. I _____ (*find*) the pen that you _____ (*lose*) yesterday. I _____ (*pick*) it up along the corridor.

7. Janet _____ (*go*) to Lake Blue. She is not here.

8. The workers _____ (*start*) work on the building several months ago and _____ just _____ (*finish*) painting it.

9. I _____ (*write*) the letter last night, and this morning I _____ (*ask*) my brother to mail it on his way to school.

10. I _____ (*tell*) them over and over not to touch my books, but they _____ (*ignore*) me.

11. A few of your friends _____ (*be*) here to see you. They _____ (*wait*) for almost an hour before they _____ (*leave*) a few minutes ago.

12. I _____ already _____ (*wait*) for an hour. He _____ (*tell*) me that I _____ (*be*) to come here at twelve o'clock, but when I _____ (*come*), he _____ (*be*) not here.

13. Recently, John _____ (*catch*) a little red squirrel. He _____ (*look*) after it carefully and _____ (*give*) it nuts to eat. He _____ (*name*) it "Red" and _____ (*adopt*) it as a pet.

PART 39

請根據提示在空格中填入合適的過去簡單式或現在完成式動詞。

1. _____ you _____ (*see*) Mary? I _____ (*promise*) to go to the exhibition with her.

2. We _____ (*not see*) that show. We _____ (*want*) to go last night but we did not get the tickets.

3. Sally _____ (*tell*) me that John _____ just _____ (*return*) from a hunting expedition, but I did not believe her.

4. My brother _____ (*buy*) a watch last month. He _____ (*use*) it for a few weeks and then _____ (*take*) it back to the shop for repairs.

5. I am afraid that I _____ (*not see*) your handkerchief. Perhaps you _____ (*drop*) it in the playground. When _____ you last _____ (*use*) it?

6. He _____ (*work*) for that company for two years. He _____ never _____ (*think*) of changing his job and _____ (*say*) that he would work there until he retires.

7. The flood that _____ (*occur*) in May _____ (*damage*) the bridge. The villagers _____ (*report*) the damage to the Township Office.

8. I _____ just _____ (*receive*) a reminder from the Electricity Board saying that we _____ (*not pay*) this month's bill. I think that they _____ (*make*) a mistake. I _____ (*pay*) the bill last week.

9. I _____ (*apply*) for a job a month ago, but I _____ (*not receive*) any reply.

10. He _____ (*tell*) me that he _____ (*live*) in this town since he was born. He _____ never _____ (*be*) away from home for more than a day.

11. She _____ finally _____ (*decide*) to join us on the trip to Sunshine Isle. She could hardly make up her mind because she _____ (*be*) there last year and _____ (*be*) not sure that she _____ (*want*) to go again this year.

12. My sister _____ (*weed*) the garden not so long ago, but the weeds _____ (*grow*) back again.

13. I'm sorry that I'm late. Nobody _____ (*tell*) me you _____ (*arrive*). _____ you _____ (*be*) here long?

14. She _____ (*say*) that she would call me this afternoon, but I _____ (*have*) no calls from her up to now. Do you think that anything _____ (*happen*) to her?

15. I _____ (*not see*) your uncle recently. Someone _____ (*tell*) me that he _____ (*go*) to Canada last month. _____ he _____ (*come*) back yet?

16. This is the first time that he _____ (*go*) to a dentist. He _____ always _____ (*be*) afraid of dentists and doctors ever since he _____ (*be*) small.

17. " _____ you _____ (*understand*) the lesson? I _____ (*prepare*) some problems for you to solve. I hope that you can do them," said the teacher.

PART 40

請根據提示在空格中填入合適的過去簡單式或現在完成式動詞。

1. We _____ (*not visit*) the zoo for many months. We _____ (*want*) to go yesterday, but we didn't because of the rain.

2. I _____ (*find*) the watch that you _____ (*lose*) yesterday but I _____ (*leave*) it at home.

3. I'm afraid that I _____ (*not see*) your cat. Perhaps it _____ (*wander*) into the neighbor's garden.

4. I _____ (*know*) him for many years, but I _____ (*not see*) him cry before.

5. She _____ just _____ (*return*) from the hospital where she _____ (*visit*) her mother.

6. This is the first time that he _____ (*go*) to a dentist. His teeth _____ always _____ (*be*) in good condition ever since he _____ (*be*) a child.

7. I _____ (*not see*) your aunt for some time. _____ she _____ (*return*) from her world trip yet? I _____ (*call*) her at the house yesterday but no one _____ (*answer*).

8. Someone _____ (*leave*) a banana peel on the pavement. Eddie _____ (*slip*) on it just now and _____ (*have*) a bad fall.

9. We _____ (*try*) to persuade her to think otherwise, but she _____ (*believe*) that she _____ (*be*) right and _____ (*refuse*) to listen to anyone.

10. The members _____ finally _____ (*agree*) to pay the increased fee. They _____ (*not want*) to do so until we _____ (*explain*) everything to them.

11. I _____ (*borrow*) a book from the library last week. I _____ (*not return*) it because I _____ (*not finish*) reading it yet.

12. She _____ (*be*) in Australia for a month, but she _____ (*not send*) us any email. She _____ (*promise*) to do so as soon as she _____ (*arrive*) there.

13. My brother _____ (*get*) a new scooter from my father. Since then, he

_____ (*seize*) every chance to show it off to his friends.

14. Two strangers _____ (*take*) shelter in front of our house just now. They _____ (*leave*) because the rain _____ (*stop*).

15. The water meter in her house _____ (*break*) down last month. She _____ (*report*) the matter to the authorities, but no one _____ (*come*) to repair it so far.

16. I _____ always _____ (*want*) to tour this country, but _____ (*have*) no time.

17. We _____ (*see*) the film last night, but they _____ (*not see*) it yet. We _____ (*enjoy*) it so much that we want to see it again.

PART 41

請根據提示在空格中填入正確的過去完成式動詞。

1. Nobody told us anything about what _____ (*happen*).

2. We could not use the road because the workmen _____ (*dig*) up parts of it.

3. After I _____ (*have*) my dinner, I started on my homework.

4. There was nothing left for me since she _____ (*take*) almost everything.

5. By the time I arrived at her house, she _____ already _____ (*go*) off.

6. He returned very late at night because a huge traffic jam _____ (*delay*) him.

7. None of us could find him because he _____ (*hide*) himself in the attic.

8. I was angry with him because he _____ (*open*) the door of the canary's cage, and it _____ (*fly*) away.

9. When Paul _____ (*finish*) building the rabbit hutch, he painted it.

10. Before they left the house, they _____ (*shut*) all the windows and _____ (*lock*) the front door.

11. No one knew exactly what _____ (*happen*) to them since no one _____ (*hear*) or _____ (*receive*) any news from them.

12. It _____ (*be*) hot in the afternoon; but it was even worse at night, and none of us _____ (*sleep*) well.

PART 42

請根據提示在空格中填入正確的過去完成式動詞。

1. She thanked me for what I _____ (*do*).

2. The meeting _____ (*start*) when he arrived.

3. I was sorry that I _____ (*upset*) his pot of paint.

4. The general praised his men for they _____ (*fight*) bravely in the battle.

5. She _____ (*not tell*) the secret to anyone else; she _____ (*keep*) it all to herself.

6. The bell _____ (*ring*) but Jimmy _____ (*not arrive*) in school yet.

7. We are lost. I wish that we _____ (*stop*) to ask the policeman for directions.

8. We _____ (*not see*) him for several years when we met him last Tuesday.

9. He asked me whether I _____ (*be*) there before. I told him that I _____ (*visit*) the place several times with my parents.

10. As soon as I _____ (*finish*) my lunch, I did my homework.

11. We _____ (*expect*) him to apologize to us for the way that he _____ (*behave*), but he didn't.

12. She discovered her mistake after she _____ (*submit*) the report. She _____ (*not be*) aware of it before.

13. We _____ (*hope*) that he would arrive on time; however, after we _____ (*wait*) for almost three hours, he still did not turn up.

PART 43

請根據提示在空格中填入合適的過去簡單式或過去完成式動詞。

1. When she _____ (*write*) the letter, she _____ (*go*) to bed.

2. By the time the ambulance _____ (*arrive*), the injured person _____ (*already die*).

3. He _____ (*tell*) me that the train _____ (*leave*) an hour before.

4. After the film _____ (*finish*), we _____ (*go*) home.

5. The dog _____ (*give*) birth to the puppies before they _____ (*realize*) it.

6. We _____ (*reach*) the airport ten minutes after we _____ (*leave*) the house.

7. Peter _____ (*say*) that he _____ (*lose*) the car keys.

8. The gardener _____ (*sweep*) up the dead leaves before we _____ (*ask*) him to do so.

9. She _____ (*lock*) her drawer after she _____ (*put*) the money inside.

10. By eight o'clock, everyone in the office _____ (*start*) to work.

11. When she _____ (*tie*) up the bags of garbage, she _____ (*throw*) them into the trash can.

12. Most of the passengers _____ (*get*) off the train when it _____ (*stop*) over at Kingston.

13. Before he _____ (*leave*), he _____ (*give*) me his address.

PART 44

請根據提示在空格中填入合適的過去簡單式或過去完成式動詞。

1. The bell _____ already _____ (*ring*) when David and Henry _____ (*reach*) school this morning.

2. Although I _____ (*be*) sure I _____ (*not see*) him before, he _____ (*look*) very familiar.

3. He _____ (*say*) that he _____ never _____ (*see*) it before, but I _____ (*know*) that he was lying.

4. The problem _____ (*prove*) to be much more difficult than any of us _____ (*think*).

5. _____ they _____ (*finish*) watering the plants before they _____ (*begin*) to cut the flowers?

6. We _____ (*be*) to that place before, but none of us could remember how to get there.

7. After he _____ (*have*) his breakfast, he _____ (*pack*) his clothes and _____ (*call*) for a taxi.

8. I _____ (*walk*) out of the shop after I _____ (*choose*) the right material and _____ (*pay*) the money.

9. The hare _____ (*run*) faster than the tortoise. When the hare _____ (*come*) to a tree by the roadside, he _____ (*rest*) for a while.

10. She _____ (*remember*) that she _____ (*not turn*) off the bathroom tap when she _____ (*be*) halfway to work.

11. When we _____ (*come*) home, we _____ (*know*) at once that something bad _____ (*happen*).

12. They _____ (*tell*) us that a man _____ (*break*) into the house when it _____ (*be*) empty and _____ (*escape*) with most of our valuables.

13. He _____ (*promise*) to return the book the next time he _____ (*come*) to my house; that _____ (*be*) why I _____ (*lend*) it to him.

14. I _____ (*trust*) him, but he _____ (*let*) me down. So, I _____ (*be*) angry with him, and I _____ (*refuse*) to speak to him.

15. I _____ (*reply*) to his letter two weeks ago, but he _____ (*never receive*) it. That _____ (*be*) why he _____ (*write*) to me again, asking why I _____ (*not reply*) to his letter.

PART 45

請根據提示在空格中填入合適的過去簡單式或過去完成式動詞。

1. He _____ (*wind*) the clock because it _____ (*stop*) during the night.

2. The laborers _____ (*tar*) only part of the road when it _____ (*start*) to rain.

3. He _____ (*search*) in his pockets, but he could not find the key. Then, he _____ (*remember*) that he _____ (*leave*) it on the dining table at home.

4. The work _____ (*prove*) to be more difficult than he _____ (*think*).

5. Although I _____ never _____ (*see*) him before, I _____ (*recognize*) him at once. My father _____ (*describe*) him very clearly to me last night.

6. We _____ (*be*) surprised to hear that he _____ (*fail*) his driving test.

7. After he _____ (*have*) his dinner, he _____ (*go*) for a walk.

8. The children _____ (*be*) exhausted when they _____ (*come*) home from the playground.

9. The police _____ (*catch*) up with him after a short chase. He _____

(*have*) no means of escape as they _____ (*handcuff*) him and _____

(*take*) him back to the police station with them.

10. After she _____ (*dust*) the furniture, she _____ (*sweep*) the floor.

11. I _____ just _____ (*go*) into the garden when I _____

(*hear*) the telephone ring. By the time I _____ (*come*) into the house and

_____ (*run*) to the phone, it _____ (*stop*) ringing.

12. The day before my brother _____ (*leave*) for Australia, we _____

(*have*) a big dinner for all our family and close friends.

13. She _____ (*hang*) all the clothes to dry when it _____ (*start*) to rain.

She _____ (*begin*) to take them in; however, after she _____ (*collect*)

all of them, the rain suddenly _____ (*stop*).

14. We _____ (*be*) exhausted by the time we _____ (*reach*) the top of the

hill.

15. I _____ (*hear*) a loud crash and _____ (*run*) out to see what

_____ (*happen*).

16. He _____ (*not know*) that his sister _____ (*come*) home from Lakeside

until he _____ (*reach*) home.

PART 46

請根據提示在空格中填入正確的未來完成式動詞。

1. The museum _____ (*close*) up for the night by the time we arrive there.

2. I _____ (*finish*) reading this story book by the end of the day.

3. You _____ (*go*) to the movies by 6: 30 at the latest, won't you?

4. _____ the children _____ (*have*) their dinner by the time we come

back?

5. The bus _____ (go) by the time you girls are ready.

6. The workmen _____ not _____ (*finish*) repairing the road by next

Monday.

7. The robbers _____ (*get*) away with the money before the police arrive.

8. Do your homework as quickly as you can, or you _____ not _____

(*finish*) it in time to watch the cartoon on television.

9. They _____ (*repair*) the computer by tomorrow. Can you collect it on your way home?

10. By the end of the year, we _____ (*have*) changed teachers three times.

11. When I finish painting this picture, I _____ (*paint*) exactly ten pictures this week.

12. Can I return the book to you tomorrow? By then, I _____ (*read*) it.

13. She _____ (*change*) a great deal since we last saw her. She _____ (*grow*) very much taller, and her manner of speaking _____ (*change*), too.

PART 47

請根據提示在空格中填入正確的未來完成式動詞。

1. By 1990, I _____ (*live*) in this town for thirty-five years.

2. Everyone _____ (*go*) to bed at this time of the night.

3. Leon Uris is a popular writer. You _____ (*hear*) of him, of course.

4. Long before your letter reaches her, she _____ (*leave*) for Europe.

5. I expect that the laborers _____ (*repair*) the bridge by the end of the week.

6. You have gone through the lesson twice. You _____ (*understand*) it better by now.

7. If we don't arrive there by six o'clock, our friends _____ (*start*) dinner without us.

8. We will get home at six o'clock. By that time the sun _____ (*set*).

9. Robert _____ (*learn*) the poem by heart before the bell rings.

10. Before you know it, he _____ (*persuade*) you to buy the car.

11. The clothes _____ (*be*) ready by then.

12. We _____ (*know*) the results of the examination by that time.

PART 48

請根據提示在空格中填入正確的現在完成進行式動詞。

1. Ever since I was small, I _____ (*live*) with my aunt.

2. She _____ (*practice*) on the piano for the last half an hour.

3. I _____ (*try*) to do this Sudoku puzzle since dinner time, and I still can't complete it.

4. I wish that someone would switch off the radio. It _____ (*play*) since this morning.

5. What _____ you _____ (*do*)? _____ you _____

(*paint*) the posters for the party?

6. I _____ (*polish*) my shoes for a long time, but they still look shabby.

7. The dog _____ (*bark*) all night. What is the matter with it?

8. I _____ (*study*) French for two years but I still can't grasp the language.

9. I _____ (*stare*) at her for some time and _____ (*try*) to recall where I have seen her.

10. You _____ (*not sleep*) well lately. _____ you _____ (*work*) too hard?

11. How long _____ she _____ (*use*) that bathroom? I _____ (*wait*) for her to finish for the last fifteen minutes.

12. I _____ (*try*) to find that book. How long _____ it _____ (*lie*) here?

13. She _____ (*shop*) the whole day, but she has bought only a skirt.

14. You must be tired. You _____ (*drive*) since morning while we _____ (*sit*) comfortably in the back.

15. My sister _____ (*water*) the plants in the garden. That's why her dress is wet. Mine is soiled because I _____ (*weed*).

16. "They _____ (*work*) since this morning. _____ you _____ (*help*) them?" he asked.

PART 49

請根據提示在空格中填入正確的現在完成進行式動詞。

1. None of the students _____ (*pay*) attention to the lesson. No wonder they don't know how to answer the teacher's questions.

2. Everyone _____ (*do*) his share of the work. They _____ (*not idle*).

3. Someone _____ (*play*) my movies. They are all disarranged.

4. The guard _____ (*work*) here for ten years and during this time, he _____ (*sleep*) in the small room behind the office.

5. She _____ (*rest*) all afternoon, yet she complains of a headache. I guess that she _____ (*read*) too long in the dim light.

6. My back is aching because I _____ (*rearrange*) the furniture in my room. Mary

_____ (*help*) me.

7. She _____ (*not feel*) well lately; that's why she _____ (*not attend*) those classes.

8. She _____ (*bake*) cakes; there's flour on her hands.

9. The police _____ (*investigate*) the case for a month, but they haven't caught anyone yet.

10. He _____ (*not take*) care of himself lately. Look, he _____ (*wear*) that shirt for a week now.

11. "_____ they _____ (*watch*) television?" "No, they _____ (*study*) in their room.

12. The students _____ (*work*) hard this term. They have done very well in the examination.

PART 50

請根據提示在空格中填入正確的現在完成進行式動詞，並在未提示的空格中依情境填入 "since" 或 "for"。

1. Mr. Brown _____ (*work*) in that firm _____ more than ten years.

2. How long _____ you _____ (*study*) at this college? _____ you _____ (*take*) courses here _____ your freshman year?

3. My mother _____ (*sew*) that frock _____ noon to get it ready for tomorrow.

4. The baby _____ (*cry*) _____ the last twenty minutes.

5. It _____ (*rain*) _____ we arrived in the town. We haven't been able to go out at all.

6. This pen _____ (*lie*) here _____ ages. I wonder whom it belongs to.

7. We _____ (*walk*) _____ more than two hours. Still we haven't arrived at the crossroads yet.

8. Mr. Penn _____ (*teach*) in this school _____ 1972.

9. "Switch off the kettle. The water _____ (*boil*) _____ three minutes already," she said.

10. I _____ (*listen*) to the lecturer _____ nearly half an hour, but I still don't know what his talk is all about.

11. Peter _____ (wear) glasses _____ he started school; he can't do without them even for a short while.

12. He is on a special diet. He _____ (eat) nothing but porridge _____ the last month.

13. What _____ you _____ (do) _____ the last time I saw you?

14. Those children _____ (play) in the rain _____ I came home.

15. Victor and Susan _____ (study) too hard _____ the last few weeks. It's time they had a rest.

16. He _____ (cough) a lot _____ he started smoking. He ought to give it up.

17. That man _____ (stand) there _____ six o'clock. I wonder if anything is wrong.

18. We _____ (use) this machine _____ years and it is still working perfectly.

PART 51

請根據提示在空格中填入合適的現在完成式或現在完成進行式動詞。

1. The mice _____ (eat) those bananas again. Look! There are several holes in them. We _____ (set) many traps, but the mice are too smart.

2. Since she started working in the office, she _____ (attend) classes to improve her shorthand.

3. He _____ (complete) his job. He deserves a rest now.

4. My brother, who _____ (be) abroad for nine years, _____ (come) back.

5. I _____ (not succeed) in waking him up. He _____ (snore) away since one o'clock.

6. He and his wife _____ (try) to buy a suitable set of furniture for their house since they shifted in.

7. The farmer _____ (wait) for the rains to come so that he can plant his crops.

8. The wind _____ (blow) strongly since noon and dark clouds _____ (gather) in the sky, but there isn't any rain at all.

9. He _____ (catch) a cold and _____ (stay) in bed since Thursday.

10. The cargo ships _____ (come) into the harbor. Many workers _____

(*unload*) the goods since this morning.

11. I'm sorry I _____ (*not pay*) attention to you. I _____ (*not sleep*) well lately, and I _____ (*feel*) ill the whole morning.

12. The police _____ (*offer*) a reward for the capture of the most wanted criminal in town. _____ you _____ (*follow*) the story of the criminal in the newspapers?

13. Someone _____ (*watch*) us all this while and he must _____ (*report*) what we _____ (*do*) since class started.

14. He _____ (*dig*) in the garden since five o'clock. He _____ (*just hear*) from a friend that treasure had been buried there during the Second World War.

PART 52

請根據提示在空格中填入合適的現在完成式或現在完成進行式動詞。

1. The baby _____ (*cry*) for a long time. Something must _____ (*disturb*) it.

2. You _____ (*sit*) here all by yourself since twelve o'clock. _____ you _____ (*have*) your lunch yet?

3. I _____ (*wait*) for her for half an hour. Perhaps she _____ (*forget*) our appointment.

4. They _____ (*avoid*) each other since the day of the party. I think something must _____ (*happen*) there.

5. Where _____ you _____ (*be*)? I _____ (*look*) for you everywhere.

6. He _____ (*go*) through everything in the house looking for his car keys. He _____ (*lose*) them somewhere.

7. They _____ (*shout*) and _____ (*yell*) at everyone since they came home. It seems they _____ (*find*) some of their money missing, and they think that one of us _____ (*take*) it.

8. The school gardener _____ (*work*) here for over seven years.

9. He _____ (*sit*) there watching television for a couple of hours. I _____ (*call*) him numerous times to come for dinner, but he _____ (*not take*) the slightest

notice.

10. What _____ Alice and Sally _____ (*do*) so long in the kitchen? I hope they _____ (*cook*) something delicious. I _____ (*be*) hungry since I came home, and the smell of food _____ (*tempt*) me all this while.

11. I _____ (*hear*) several stories about the new girl. It seems that she _____ just _____ (*recover*) from a serious illness and her parents sent her here, hoping that the sea air will be good for her.

PART 53

請根據提示在空格中填入合適的現在完成式或現在完成進行式動詞。

1. We _____ (*wait*) here for an hour, but Toby _____ (*not turn*) up yet.

2. The police _____ (*look*) for him in vain. Everybody says they _____ (*not see*) him.

3. He _____ (*read*) *War and Peace* all day long. That is why he _____ (*neglect*) his homework.

4. "I _____ (*hear*) about him, but I _____ never _____ (*meet*) him."

5. We _____ (*stand*) here for some time, but we _____ (*not notice*) anything suspicious.

6. "Allen, you _____ (*whisper*) to your neighbor for the last ten minutes. I _____ (*watch*) you all the time."

7. They _____ (*have*) no electricity since the storm destroyed the wires.

8. He _____ (*lose*) his wallet and _____ (*try*) to find it, but he _____ (*have*) no success so far.

9. The cigarette butt is still warm. Someone _____ (*smoke*) here and _____ just _____ (*leave*).

10. This book _____ (*lie*) on my desk for days. _____ you _____ (*check*) to see if it's yours?

11. Elsie _____ (*come*) back from the United Kingdom. She _____ (*visit*) all her friends since.

12. I _____ (*walk*) three kilometers, but _____ (*not see*) a single house

yet.

13. She _____ (*sew*) all morning. How _____ you _____ (*spend*) your morning?

14. Somebody _____ (*play*) with my bicycle bell. I _____ (*hear*) it ringing from my room.

15. My brother _____ (*read*) my book and _____ (*take*) out my bookmark.

16. "Finally! Everyone else _____ (*give*) up hope that you would turn up. Nevertheless, we _____ (*wait*) for you."

PART 54

請根據提示在空格中填入合適的現在完成式或現在完成進行式動詞。

1. The committee _____ (*discuss*) the issue all morning, but they _____ (*not reach*) a decision yet.

2. She _____ (*work*) for him for ten years and she _____ never _____ (*meet*) a more considerate employer.

3. Mr. Robinson _____ (*think*) of emigrating to Canada, but he _____ (*not make*) any definite plans yet.

4. She _____ (*learn*) to cook many new dishes, but she _____ (*not put*) what she _____ (*learn*) into practice yet.

5. I _____ (*not see*) you for a long time. What _____ you _____ (*do*)?

6. She _____ (*not be*) here since November. I don't know what _____ (*happen*) to her.

7. I _____ (*look*) at the photograph of the twins for the past ten minutes, and I _____ (*not be*) able to tell who is who.

8. We _____ (*fish*) near the waterfall all day, and we _____ (*not have*) a decent meal at all.

9. Fanny _____ (*practice*) on the piano the whole morning. No one _____ (*interrupt*) her playing.

10. I _____ (*know*) them for some time now, but I _____ never

_____ (*visit*) them at their house.

11. That clock _____ (*hang*) there for as long as I can remember. It _____ (*not break*) down even once and it _____ (*show*) the correct time, too.

12. They _____ (*concentrate*) so much on winning the trophy that they _____ (*neglect*) their studies.

PART 55

請根據提示在空格中填入合適的現在完成式或現在完成進行式動詞。

1. He _____ (*think*) of a solution to the problem, but he _____ (*not think*) out any possible ways of overcoming it yet.

2. We _____ (*fish*) all afternoon, but we _____ (*not catch*) any fish yet.

3. They _____ always _____ (*dislike*) that man and recently they _____ (*try*) to stay out of his way.

4. That child _____ (*eat*) candies the whole morning. She _____ (*eat*) all the candies you bought for her.

5. If you _____ (*not understand*) the lesson, you must _____ (*sleep*) in class.

6. I _____ (*work*) in the garden all day and I _____ (*not see*) anyone come in through the gate.

7. It _____ (*not rain*) since last month and the stream _____ (*dry*) up.

8. I _____ (*observe*) him since he came to work here. I _____ (*notice*) that he is intelligent as well as diligent.

9. Bobby _____ (*watch*) television since he returned from school. He _____ (*not have*) his bath or dinner yet.

PART 56

請根據提示在空格中填入合適的現在完成式或現在完成進行式動詞。

1. He _____ (*save*) up his money since last year, and now he _____ (*save*) enough to go to Europe for a holiday.

2. The cat _____ (*mew*) at the door for the past hour. _____ you _____ (*feed*) him yet?

3. The pipe _____ (*leak*) since yesterday, but we _____ (*not call*) in the plumber yet.

4. The statue _____ (*stand*) here for centuries, and now the government _____ (*decide*) to move it to the museum.

5. She _____ (*not buy*) any new clothes since last year as she _____ (*be*) busy all this while.

6. They _____ (*build*) the bridge for nearly a year, but they _____ (*not complete*) it yet.

7. Although my cousins _____ (*study*) overseas for five years, they _____ (*not obtain*) their degrees yet.

8. He _____ (*not have*) a rest since the shop opened.

9. _____ he _____ (*forget*) to bring his pen again? I _____ (*remind*) him about it for the past few days, but it _____ (*be*) of no use at all.

PART 57

請根據提示在空格中填入正確的過去完成進行式動詞。

1. She _____ (*cry*) since she discovered that her cat was missing.

2. We _____ (*hike*) for the past few days; that is why we look so exhausted.

3. The boys said that they _____ (*fish*) in that river for over three hours.

4. He _____ (*stare*) at her when he realized that she was someone he knew.

5. These people _____ (*work*) in that factory until they were suddenly dismissed for incompetence.

6. _____ they _____ (*write*) to each other until they quarreled the other day in Mary's house?

7. The workmen _____ (*build*) those houses for over two months.

8. He _____ (*sit*) there, daydreaming, until I asked him to join the game.

9. Before he made that trip into the jungle last month, he _____ (*do*) a lot of research work.

10. I _____ (*help*) my mother the whole day yesterday. That was why I went to bed so early.

11. After I _____ (*use*) it for a number of months, I discovered that it was not genuine

at all.

12. You would have had better marks on the examination if you _____ (*study*) hard for the past year.

PART 58

請根據提示在空格中填入正確的過去完成進行式動詞。

1. The teacher punished her because she _____ (*not pay*) attention at all during the lesson.

2. He _____ just _____ (*tell*) us all about his adventure in foreign lands.

3. The grumpy old woman opened the door after we _____ (*knock*) for some time.

4. _____ she _____ (*play*) with the paint? Her hands and face had paint all over them.

5. My sister _____ (*not read*) at all. She _____ (*sleep*) all that while.

6. I told him that he _____ (*not talk*) unnecessarily, but he wouldn't believe me.

7. He suffered from gastric pains because he _____ (*not take*) regular meals.

8. She _____ (*not think*) about the problem, or else she would have given us an answer.

9. He _____ (*pester*) his father to buy him a motorcycle for his eighteenth birthday.

10. All those who _____ (*spread*) false rumors were warned to stop doing so.

11. She _____ (*eat*) nothing but porridge ever since her illness.

12. _____ his mother _____ (*support*) him all the time? He should have got himself a job.

PART 59

請根據提示在空格中填入正確的過去完成進行式動詞。

1. The alarm clock _____ (*ring*) for some time before he woke up.

2. I _____ (*look*) forward to meeting her ever since you described her to me.

3. She looked distraught. _____ someone _____ (*scold*) her?

4. The children _____ (*splash*) about in that shallow pond since morning.

5. We _____ just _____ (*talk*) about him when he entered the room.

6. Mrs. Wilson _____ (*teach*) for more than twenty years before she retired.

7. We discovered that we had lost our way after we _____ (*drive*) around for some time.

8. After I _____ (*search*) for it the whole day, I found it hidden among some books.

9. She _____ (*write*) for ten minutes before her pen ran out of ink.

10. The notebook computer was not working, and she suspected that the boys _____ (*meddle*) with it.

11. He _____ (*stay*) with his grandparents ever since the floods had washed his house away.

12. They _____ (*paint*) the house the whole day and they badly needed a rest.

Chapter 11 語　態

11-0 基本概念

在英文文法中，語態是相當重要的，大部分的動詞都有主動與被動的用法，同時也都可以被應用在各種時態中。主動語態使用正常的句子結構，表示「由主詞所執行的動作」，行為者（主詞）和動作缺一不可；被動語態則表示「某動作發生在主詞身上」，強調動作和承受者（主詞），真正的行為者甚至可以被省略。

11-1 被動語態的形式

(a) 被動語態的形式主要是「be 動詞 + 過去分詞」。換句話說，一個動詞的被動式是由適當的 be 動詞，加上該動詞的過去分詞所構成。這其中，會因時態而改變的只有前面的 be 動詞，後面的過去分詞是不會改變的。

USAGE PRACTICE		
	主　動	被　動
現在簡單式	I teach. 我教。	**I am taught.** 我被教。
現在進行式	I am teaching. 我正在教。	**I am being taught.** 我正在被教。
現在完成式	I have taught. 我已經教了。	**I have been taught.** 我已經被教了。

小練習

請根據提示在空格中填入正確的被動語態（請用現在簡單式或現在進行式）。

1. My typewriter _____ (*be repairing*) at the moment. The spare one _____ (*spoil*), so I have to borrow yours.

2. This road _____ (*not be using*) by motorists because the bridge _____ (*be repairing*).

3. Everyone _____ (*expect*) to keep quiet when the examination results _____ (*be announcing*).

4. You _____ (*tell*) to send in your application forms by next Monday. You must hurry; even now other applications _____ (*be considering*).

5. Every student _____ (*give*) a chance to read aloud in class. Now, the passage _____ (*be reading*) by Maria.

6. The fruits _____ (*be taking*) to the factory. There they _____ (*peel*), _____ (*wash*), _____ (*cook*), and _____ (*can*) all by machines.

7. The children _____ (*take*) to school by their father every morning. They _____ always _____ (*leave*) at the school gate.

8. The people _____ (*warn*) not to give shelter to the escaped convict. The warning _____ (*print*) in all newspapers and _____ (*be broadcasting*) over radio and television.

9. The cabinets here _____ (*not be using*) because they _____ (*spoil*). At present, the files _____ (*keep*) in those cabinets.

10. Do you see the bales of cotton that _____ (*be loading*) on to the ship? Cotton _____ (*export*) to other countries in large quantities.

11. Pepper _____ (*grow*) in that region and _____ (*export*) to many countries. Now, steps _____ (*be taking*) by farmers to increase their production.

12. The clothes _____ (*be washing*) now. You had better see that the clothesline _____ (*put*) up.

13. This film _____ (*produce*) by the Super Whizz Organization and now _____ (*be showing*) in many of the movie theaters all over the world.

14. The bad news _____ (*be keeping*) as a secret from the old lady. It _____ (*fear*) that she may die of shock if she hears it.

15. Do you see those guards? They _____ (*station*) there to check everyone who passes through. Look, that man's luggage _____ (*be searching*) now.

16. The library _____ (*be cleaning*) now. No one _____ (*allow*) to enter it.

17. The parts of these machines _____ (*make*) in Japan but _____ (*assemble*) here. However, now some parts _____ (*be making*) locally.

18. It _____ (*hope*) that our standard of living will improve. At the moment, steps _____ (*be taking*) to create jobs for the unemployed.

19. There is a long line at the counter where stamps _____ (*be selling*). In the near

future, we won't have to wait so long because a new office _____ (*be building*) to serve the area.

☞ 更多相關習題請見本章應用練習 Part 1。

11-2 被動語態的用法

(a) 當動作或動作的承受者比行為者重要時，可以用被動語態強調其重要性。

USAGE PRACTICE	
主　動	被　動
▶ People sell his books all over the world. 人們在世界各地販賣他的書。	▶ His books **are sold** all over the world. 他的書在世界各地被販賣。
▶ They will serve dinner at seven o'clock. 他們將在七點提供晚餐。	▶ Dinner **will be served** at seven o'clock. 晚餐將在七點提供。
▶ The guard had locked the gate last night. 這警衛昨晚已把大門鎖上。	▶ The gate **had been locked** last night. 大門昨晚已被鎖上。
▶ Somebody had left the windows open last night. 昨晚有人讓窗戶開著沒關。	▶ The windows **had been left** open last night. 昨晚窗戶被打開著。
▶ They have sold the painting already. 他們已經把這幅賣掉了。	▶ The painting **has been sold** already. 這幅畫已經被賣掉了。
▶ The workers load the logs of wood onto trucks. 工人把圓木裝上卡車。	▶ The logs of wood **are loaded** onto trucks. 圓木被裝上卡車。
▶ They will hold an art exhibition on Saturday. 他們將於週六辦藝術展。	▶ An art exhibition **will be held** on Saturday. 藝術展將在週六舉行。
▶ They use leather to make these shoes. 他們用皮革做成這些鞋子。	▶ These shoes **are made** of leather. 這些鞋子是用皮革做成的。
▶ He told me not to sit there. 他告訴我不要坐在那裡。	▶ I **was told** not to sit there. 我被告知不要坐在那裡。

(b) 當不確定行為者的身分時，多用被動語態表示「動作的發生」。

USAGE PRACTICE

主　動	被　動
▶ Someone has stolen my camera. 有人偷了我的相機。	▶ My camera **has been stolen**. 我的相機被偷了。
▶ Somebody opens the door every morning. 每天早上有人開門。	▶ The door **is opened** every morning. 每天早上門被打開。
▶ Someone kidnapped the guard yesterday. 昨天有人綁架了警衛。	▶ The guard **was kidnapped** yesterday. 昨天警衛被綁架了。
▶ Someone found the purse outside the hall. 有人在大廳外發現這個皮包。	▶ The purse **was found** outside the hall. 這個皮包在大廳外被發現。
▶ People mustn't take this book out of the library. 人們不可把這本書拿到圖書館外面。	▶ This book **mustn't be taken** out of the library. 這本書不可被拿到圖書館外面。
▶ Somebody swept the floor yesterday. 昨天有人掃地。	▶ The floor **was swept** yesterday. 昨天地板被掃了。
▶ The guests will park their cars by the roadside. 客人們會將車子停在路旁。	▶ The cars **will be parked** by the roadside. 車子會被停在路旁。
▶ People use the library six days a week. 人們一週有六天使用圖書館。	▶ The library **is used** six days a week. 圖書館一週有六天被使用。
▶ People speak English everywhere. 到處有人說英文。	▶ English **is spoken** everywhere. 英文到處被說。
▶ They did not harm the Red Cross members. 他們沒有傷害紅十字會的人員。	▶ The Red Cross members **were not harmed**. 紅十字會的人員沒有被傷害。
▶ They will send him to jail. 他們將把他送進監獄。	▶ He **will be sent** to jail. 他將被送進監獄。
▶ Someone delivered the goods to the house last night. 昨晚有人將這批貨物遞送到府。	▶ The goods **were delivered** to the house last night. 這批貨物昨晚被遞送到府。

(c) 但是，有時為了使句意完整，動作者有被提及的必要，即在被動語態後加上「by + 行為者」。

USAGE PRACTICE	
主　動	被　動
▶ A truck hit him yesterday. 昨天有一部卡車撞到他。	▶ He **was hit** by a truck yesterday. 昨天他被一部卡車撞到。
▶ A car had run over him. 一輛車輾過他。	▶ He **had been run over** by a car. 他被一輛車輾過。
▶ Arthur Hill produced and presented the program. 亞瑟・希爾製作並出品這個節目。	▶ The program **was produced** and **presented** by Arthur Hill. 這個節目被亞瑟・希爾製作並出品。
▶ Shakespeare wrote the play *Hamlet*. 莎士比亞寫了《哈姆雷特》這齣戲。	▶ The play *Hamlet* **was written** by Shakespeare. 《哈姆雷特》這齣戲是由莎士比亞所寫。
▶ Johann Strauss composed this piece of music. 約翰・史特勞斯寫了這首樂曲。	▶ This piece of music **was composed** by Johann Strauss. 這首樂曲是約翰・史特勞斯寫的。
▶ The same person signed these two documents. 同一個人簽署了這兩份文件。	▶ These two documents **were signed** by the same person. 這兩份文件被同一個人簽署。
▶ The sight of the stranger frightened her. 她一看見那個陌生人就害怕。	▶ She **was frightened** by the sight of the stranger. 看見那個陌生人，她被嚇到了。
▶ Skilled artisans make these delicate watches. 熟練的工匠製造了這些精緻的手錶。	▶ These delicate watches **are made** by skilled artisans. 這些精緻的手錶由熟練的工匠製造。
▶ The secretary drew up the company's annual report. 秘書擬定了公司的年度報告。	▶ The company's annual report **was drawn up** by the secretary. 公司的年度報告是由秘書擬定。

小練習

請用被動語態改寫下列句子，如有必要則須寫出動作者。

1. We bake the cookies over a charcoal fire.

$\rightarrow$ _____

2. The secretary will write the minutes of the meeting.

$\rightarrow$ _____

3. They have discussed the problem for several days.

$\rightarrow$ _____

4. Somebody has switched on the radio.

$\rightarrow$ _____

5. They built that block of flats in 1973.

$\rightarrow$ _____

6. They beat our team in the hockey match yesterday.

$\rightarrow$ _____

7. We often find flies near rubbish dumps.

$\rightarrow$ _____

8. Somebody broke into our house last night.

$\rightarrow$ _____

9. Robert Browning wrote the poem, "The Pied Piper of Hamelin."

$\rightarrow$ _____

10. "Did anyone tell you where to report for work?" "No, no one told me."

$\rightarrow$ _____

11. The earthquake destroyed many buildings and killed many people.

$\rightarrow$ _____

12. We can find many types of seashells along the seashore. Many people visit this place during the school holidays.

$\rightarrow$ _____

13. Someone has discovered iron ore on the tiny island. They have sent an expert there to investigate.

$\rightarrow$ _____

14. You should peel the skins of the potatoes before you cook them.

$\rightarrow$ _____

☞ 更多相關習題請見本章應用練習 Part 2～Part 8。

11-3 授與動詞的被動語態

(a) 授與動詞有兩個受詞，即直接受詞與間接受詞，一般多用間接受詞（表示「人」的受詞）作主詞。

USAGE PRACTICE	
主　動	被　動
▶ Someone gave me a watch. 有人給我一隻錶。	▶ I **was given** a watch. 我被給了一隻錶。
▶ The man told her an interesting story. 這男人告訴她一個有趣的故事。	▶ She **was told** an interesting story. 她被告知一個有趣的故事。
▶ They presented him with a prize for being the best speaker. 他們因為他是最佳的演講者而頒獎給他。	▶ He **was presented** with a prize for being the best speaker. 他因為是最佳演講者而獲獎。

(b) 直接受詞也可以當主詞，作為強調。然而，這種用法較少見。

USAGE PRACTICE	
主　動	被　動
▶ They sent the letter to him on Monday. 他們星期一把這封信送交給他。	▶ The letter **was sent to** him on Monday. 這封信在星期一被送交給他。
▶ Someone gave her a watch. 有人給她一隻錶。	▶ A watch **was given** to her. 一隻錶被給她。
▶ The manager offered him a job in the company. 經理提供他一份這公司的工作。	▶ A job in the company **was offered** to him. 一份在這公司的工作被提供給他。

 小練習

請將粗體部分作為主詞，用被動語態改寫下列句子。

1. Someone told **me** a very sad story about her.

→ _____

2. They gave **me** the wrong change at the shop.

→ _____

3. They have given **women in most countries** the right to vote.

→ _____

4. We shall give them **a set of silver cutlery** on their silver wedding anniversary.

→ _____

5. Someone has promised **him** a reward if he finds the dog.

→ _____

6. They asked **the lecturer** a very difficult question.

→ _____

7. No one will tell **him** the truth about the situation.

→ _____

8. They offered him **a job**, but he turned **it** down.

→ _____

9. They are giving each child **a second serving of ice cream**.

→ _____

10. Someone gave him **an autograph book** to sign.

→ _____

11-4 含有介系詞的被動語態

(a) 當一個句子由主動語態改成被動語態時，絕不可以省略片語動詞中的介系詞或介副詞。

USAGE PRACTICE	
主　動	被　動
▶ Somebody locked the dog out last night. 昨晚有人將這隻狗鎖在外面。	▶ The dog **was locked out** last night. 這隻狗昨晚被鎖在外面。
▶ She will look after you well. 她會好好照顧你。	▶ You **will be looked after** well. 你會被好好照顧。
▶ They gossiped about her all over the village. 他們在村子裡到處講她的八卦。	▶ She **was gossiped about** all over the village. 她被人在村子裡到處講八卦。
▶ They left her behind by mistake. 他們陰錯陽差把她留在原地。	▶ She **was left behind** by mistake. 她陰錯陽差被留在原地。

▶ They have found out the truth.	▶ The truth **has been found out**.
他們已經找出真相。	真相已經被找出了。
▶ They must look into this matter.	▶ This matter **must be looked into**.
他們必須深入調查這件事。	這件事必須被深入調查。
▶ They have brought him up strictly.	▶ He **has been brought up** strictly.
他們已嚴格地把他撫養長大。	他已經被嚴格地撫養長大。

小練習

請用被動語態改寫下列句子。

1. They will take care of the child properly.

   → _____

2. Someone is conducting research into the private life of that great sculptor.

   → _____

3. They will deal with these problems one at a time.

   → _____

4. They took down the old notice, and they put up another one in its place.

   → _____

5. The teacher ordered Tom out of the classroom because he was making too much noise.

   → _____

6. They left the hall lights on in case they decided to come back that night.

   → _____

7. Someone locked the detective in while he was absorbed in examining something.

   → _____

8. My uncle pointed out the landmarks of the town to me.

   → _____

9. When they were halfway there, they suddenly realized that they had left Emily behind.

   → _____

10. The little boys who were playing in the garden this morning have messed up all my washing.

   → _____

11-5 其他形式的被動語態

(a) 動詞是 say、think、fear、claim、believe、assume、consider、understand 等的直述句由主動語態改成被動語態時，其句子結構必須改變，被動語態後接不定詞。

USAGE PRACTICE	
主　動	被　動
▶ People say that he is mad. 　人們說他瘋了。	▶ He **is said** to be mad. 　他被說是瘋了。
▶ People say that women are the weaker sex. 人們說女人是弱者。	▶ Women **are said** to be the weaker sex. 　女人被說是弱者。
▶ People think that smoking is bad for health. 人們認為吸煙對健康有害。	▶ Smoking **is thought** to be bad for health. 　吸煙被認為對健康有害。
▶ They believe that the old warrior is still alive. 他們相信這老戰士還活著。	▶ The old warrior **is believed** to be still alive. 據信這老戰士還活著。
▶ People believe that he had been murdered by his rivals. 　人們相信他已經被他的敵手謀殺了。	▶ He **is believed** to have been murdered by his rivals. 　據信他已經被他的敵手謀殺了。
▶ They believed that she is an heiress to a large fortune. 　他們相信她是一大筆財富的繼承人。	▶ She **is believed** to be an heiress to a large fortune. 　據信她是一大筆財富的繼承人。
▶ Somebody saw him open the door. 　有人看見他開門。	▶ He **was seen** to open the door. 　他被看見開門。
▶ They know that she has failed it. 　他們知道她失敗了。	▶ She **is known** to have failed it. 　她被得知失敗了。
▶ People knew that he went there often. 　人們知道他經常去那裡。	▶ He **was known** to go there often. 　他被得知經常去那裡。
▶ People consider him to have the most land in the village. 　人們認為他在村子裡擁有最多的土地。	▶ He **is considered** to have the most land in the village. 　他被認為在村子裡擁有最多的土地。
▶ They claim that their fields yield the most wheat in the world.　他們宣稱他們的農田生產世界上最多的小麥。	▶ Their fields **are claimed** to yield the most wheat in the world. 　他們的農田被宣稱生產世界上最多的小麥。

▶ We assume that the factor remains constant. 我們假定這個因素保持不變。	▶ The factor **is assumed** to remain constant. 這個因素被假定保持不變。
▶ We fear that the child has been lost in the flood. 我們害怕那個小孩已在洪水中失蹤了。	▶ The child **is feared** to have been lost in the flood. 那個小孩恐怕已在洪水中失蹤了。

(b) 這些動詞在改為被動語態時，也常改為 "It is/was..." 的形式。

USAGE PRACTICE	
主　動	被　動
▶ People fear that there will be another world war. 人們害怕將會有另一次世界大戰。	▶ **It is feared** that there will be another world war. 恐怕將會有另一次世界大戰。
▶ They fear that there are no survivors. 他們害怕沒有生還者。	▶ **It is feared** that there are no survivors. 恐怕沒有生還者。
▶ They say that there are ghosts in that old house. 他們說那棟老房子裡有鬼。	▶ **It is said** that there are ghosts in that old house. 據說那棟老房子裡有鬼。
▶ They assumed that there was no more food left. 他們假定沒有剩餘的食物。	▶ **It was assumed** that there was no more food left. 假定沒有剩餘的食物。
▶ They no longer believe that the earth is flat. 他們再也不相信地球是平的。	▶ **It is** no longer **believed** that the earth is flat. 再也沒人相信地球是平的。

(c) 感官動詞或使役動詞在主動語態中，後接原形動詞（感官動詞也可接現在分詞）；
但是，在被動語態中，後面要接不定詞。

USAGE PRACTICE	
主　動	被　動
▶ Somebody saw her climb through the window. 有人看到她爬過窗戶。	▶ She **was seen** to climb through the window. 她被看到爬過窗戶。
▶ Someone heard him threatening the schoolboy. 有人聽到他脅迫學童。	▶ He **was heard** to be threatening the schoolboy. 他被聽到脅迫學童。

▶ They <u>made</u> him <u>work</u> like a slave.	▶ He **was made** to work like a slave.
他們強使他像奴隸般工作。	他被迫像奴隸般工作。

請將粗體部分作為主詞，用被動語態改寫下列句子。

1. People consider **him** to be the richest man in the country.

   → _____

2. They say that **these herbs** are good for rheumatism.

   → _____

3. We think that **she** is the most understanding and patient teacher in the school.

   → _____

4. They thought that **the boy** was joking when he mentioned his part in the tragedy.

   → _____

5. People believed that **witches from nearby villages** met in the woods when the moon was full.

   → _____

6. People said that **he** married his wife while he was abroad.

   → _____

7. People know that **he** is a wanted man.

   → _____

8. People say that **blood** is always thicker than water.

   → _____

9. People believed that **he** was the strongest man living.

   → _____

10. They claimed that **the product** was the best on the market.

    → _____

11. They say that **the Vikings** discovered America first.

    → _____

12. People generally assume that **fat people** are lazy.

    → _____

13. Somebody saw **him** committing the crime.

→ _____

14. Someone saw **her** take a letter out of the letter box.

→ _____

15. Something makes **the light** pass through a filter.

→ _____

16. Someone saw **him** teasing the dog with a bone.

→ _____

☞ 更多相關習題請見本章應用練習 Part 9～Part 13。

Chapter 11　應用練習

PART 1

請根據提示在空格中填入正確的被動語態（請用現在簡單式或現在進行式）。

1. The students _____ (*forbid*) to enter the library because it _____ (*be repainting*) at the moment.

2. Do you see the rubber sheets that _____ (*pack*) in bales? They _____ (*be loading*) on the ship now.

3. The script _____ (*write*) by Mr. White and the songs _____ (*compose*) by his wife. We do not know who will be in the cast yet; the actors _____ (*be selecting*) now.

4. The washing machine _____ (*not be using*) at present because it has broken down. It _____ (*be repairing*) now.

5. The goods _____ (*import*) from the United States. They _____ (*distribute*) by various agencies but attempts _____ (*be making*) to produce them locally.

6. Accidents often occur because of careless driving. Frequently, the guilty driver _____ (*sue*) by the other driver who _____ (*involve*) in the accident.

7. Traffic _____ (*expect*) to flow more smoothly when work on widening the highway _____ (*complete*).

8. "I think that I _____ (*be following*) by a man who _____ (*want*) by the police," he said.

9. A warning sign _____ (*place*) near the big tree that _____ (*be cutting*) down now. Motorists _____ (*be diverting*) by the police to another road.

10. The goods in the window of the shop _____ (*be arranging*) at the moment. Customers _____ (*invite*) to look at other parts of the shop.

11. Preparations _____ (*be making*) to build houses there. Bulldozers _____ (*be bringing*) in and the land _____ (*be leveling*) now.

12. Nancy's car _____ (*park*) outside the tailor's shop. She _____ (*be measuring*) by the tailor for a dress now.

13. The damaged car _____ (*be towing*) by a truck to the workshop now.

14. The two suspects _____ (*be interrogating*) by the police at the moment. They _____ (*be holding*) in custody until bail _____ (*arrange*) for them.

15. The prize-giving ceremony _____ usually _____ (*watch*) by more than four hundred people. The head prefect _____ always _____ (*present*) with a medal.

16. The candidates for the job _____ (*be interviewing*) by the manager now. Then, they _____ (*give*) a test to find out whether they are suitable for the job.

17. The plane _____ (*schedule*) to arrive at the airport at five o'clock and _____ (*expect*) to depart for Tokyo at six.

18. The houses _____ (*not occupy*) as the certificates of fitness _____ (*not issue*) yet.

PART 2

請用被動語態改寫下列句子（不要寫出動作者）。

1. They have informed the guards to watch the gate closely.

    → _____

2. The maid showed her into a large hall.

    → _____

3. The gardener uses the dried grass as fertilizer.

    → _____

4. People must do something for these poor children.

    → _____

5. Somebody locks the gates every night.

→ _____

6. Workers are pulling down the old building.

→ _____

7. You must not expose the film to sunlight.

→ _____

8. Someone should inform the district officer about the state of affairs here.

→ _____

9. Did anyone tell you to keep it a secret?

→ _____

10. The laborers carry the bunches of oil-palm fruit to the waiting truck.

→ _____

11. Why didn't anybody tell me about the change of plans?

→ _____

12. People spend far more money on food than on any other thing.

→ _____

13. You ought to keep these things out of children's reach.

→ _____

14. We will say nothing more about the matter if someone returns the stolen jewels.

→ _____

15. The police used dogs to track down the escaped criminals.

→ _____

16. They had built an enormous dam to keep back the water.

→ _____

17. No one can do anything to help you if you don't cooperate.

→ _____

PART 3

請用被動語態改寫下列句子，如有必要則須寫出動作者。

1. The doctor gave him an injection and some pills.

→ _____

2. A blow on the chin struck him down.

→ _____

3. Has the fire destroyed a large part of the building?

→ _____

4. Byron couldn't have written the poem.

→ _____

5. The Governor had opened the new State Secretariat.

→ _____

6. People must write the answers on one side of the paper only.

→ _____

7. You can tell that the same person wrote these two letters.

→ _____

8. They fought a big battle here many years ago.

→ _____

9. Did his manner impress the manager?

→ _____

10. The large reward attracted him.

→ _____

11. People will admire you for your courage and determination.

→ _____

12. A flash of lightning lit up the room for a second.

→ _____

13. Complete silence succeeded the shot.

→ _____

14. No one can ever answer this question satisfactorily.

→ _____

15. People wore these shells as a protection against evil spirits.

→ _____

16. The closure of the factory would render a lot of men jobless.

→ _____

17. A slight increase in pressure will break the tubing.

→ _____

18. Someone has opened the lock and taken out all the money.

→ _____

19. They tell me that the judge had sentenced him to five years in jail.

→ _____

20. Nobody can pronounce you guilty until they have proved that you are.

→ _____

PART 4

請用被動語態改寫下列句子，如有必要則須寫出動作者。

1. You should check the figures carefully.

→ _____

2. Somebody found a wallet and some important documents near the bus stop.

→ _____

3. We use the refrigerator to keep vegetables and fruit cool and fresh.

→ _____

4. No one has ever beaten him in archery.

→ _____

5. Some people are requesting the film star to sign some autographs right now.

→ _____

6. The police chief himself praised the man for catching the thief.

→ _____

7. An Italian named Christopher Columbus discovered America.

→ _____

8. We will dust all the furniture before we sweep the house.

→ _____

9. They had certainly locked the door when they left the house this morning.

→ _____

10. They should not have built the village on the riverbank. When the river floods, it will sweep the village away.

→ _____

11. Lightning struck the huge tree and sent it toppling down on the house.

→ _____

12. They rebuilt their house, and their neighbors helped them out with gifts of food, clothes and furniture.

→ _____

13. The swallows have made the place dirty. Someone removes their nests and cleans up the place.

→ _____

14. They said that the girl was missing, so they organized a search party. They found her lying unconscious in a deep ditch and brought her home.

→ _____

PART 5

請用被動語態改寫下列句子，如有必要則須寫出動作者。

1. Someone stole some top-secret documents from the Secretariat.

→ _____

2. No one has used the building for the last fifty years.

→ _____

3. People will forget this incident in a few years' time.

→ _____

4. No one has ever taken him at his word.

→ _____

5. You must not take the joke too seriously.

→ _____

6. She hurt her leg in the match.

→ _____

7. They fought a bitter battle here years ago.

→ _____

8. Someone told them to go away.

→ _____

9. Someone should hang the bunting up before the carnival starts.

→ _____

10. They took the prisoners away in a van.

→ _____

11. Everyone must obey the traffic regulations.

→ _____

12. They asked her to finish the work.

→ _____

13. People in all parts of the world play football.

→ _____

14. Nobody will reveal the truth about the situation.

→ _____

15. He had not touched the jewels.

→ _____

16. Will they round up the cattle?

→ _____

17. Who can repair this broken chair?

→ _____

18. They will laugh at you for asking such a question.

→ _____

19. Everyone will think that you are foolish.

→ _____

20. Will somebody show the visitors around the garden?

→ _____

PART 6

請用被動語態改寫下列句子，如有必要則須寫出動作者。

1. A truck ran over the dog.

→ _____

2. Someone switched off the lights.

→ _____

3. Did someone find a solution to the problem?

→ _____

4. The blind man has made the chair very well.

→ _____

5. An unseen hand closed the window.

→ _____

6. Beethoven composed this lovely piece of music.

→ _____

7. What were they loading on to the truck?

→ _____

8. They still deny women the right to vote in some countries.

→ _____

9. Did the uproar frighten you?

→ _____

10. A gigantic wave overturned the frail boat.

→ _____

11. They shouldn't treat me as if I were a child!

→ _____

12. Somebody has locked the chest, and I can't open it.

→ _____

13. Didn't they tell you to be here by three o'clock?

→ _____

14. The judge gave the thief a fair trial and sent him to prison for two years.

→ _____

15. Her misery affected me deeply.

→ _____

PART 7

請用被動語態改寫下列句子，如有必要則須寫出動作者。

1. People speak English all over the world.

→ _____

2. People will forget this scandal in time to come.

→ _____

3. Someone can easily repair this machine.

   → _____

4. Someone left this parcel here for you.

   → _____

5. Has anyone cleaned the room yet?

   → _____

6. No one told us anything about the change of venue.

   → _____

7. They ordered the prisoners to turn to face the wall.

   → _____

8. Someone made this carpet in Iran.

   → _____

9. He painted the portrait beautifully.

   → _____

10. Someone will take you to the manager's office.

   → _____

11. They should repair this road as soon as possible.

   → _____

12. He is asking the girl to show her passport.

   → _____

13. He made over the estate to the orphanage.

   → _____

14. People will take this statement to be the truth.

   → _____

15. The cat licked up the spilled milk.

   → _____

PART 8

請用被動語態改寫下列句子，如有必要則須寫出動作者。

1. They held a party to celebrate their victory.

   → _____

2. The fire destroyed many houses.

→ _____

3. Someone will lead the blind man across the street.

→ _____

4. Why has nobody done anything about this matter?

→ _____

5. They will hand in their essays tomorrow.

→ _____

6. People always speak well of that doctor.

→ _____

7. What questions did the interviewer ask you?

→ _____

8. The police have tracked down the criminal.

→ _____

9. They asked the boy to do a very difficult task.

→ _____

10. The headwaiter himself showed us to our table.

→ _____

11. They will elect a new president of the club.

→ _____

12. He can't shut the door properly.

→ _____

13. Jack beat John in the 100-meter race.

→ _____

14. Someone has misplaced the book. I can't find it anywhere.

→ _____

15. Leonardo da Vinci painted the *Mona Lisa*.

→ _____

16. They told me that someone had broken into your house.

→ _____

PART 9

請用 "It is/was..." 的型態將下列句子改寫為被動語態。

1. The natives believe that evil spirits cause illnesses.

   → _____

2. They believe that there are many horizons man can explore.

   → _____

3. They fear that all the passengers in the ship were drowned.

   → _____

4. They say that there is great potential wealth in the oceans.

   → _____

5. They assumed that the answer was correct.

   → _____

6. They know that she is innocent of the crime.

   → _____

7. They considered him the most brilliant of all the men there.

   → _____

8. They claimed that their car was damaged in the accident.

   → _____

9. People fear that the Third World War will break out in this generation.

   → _____

10. They knew that the thief always struck at night.

    → _____

11. People think that the rite is out-dated.

    → _____

12. They understand that speeding is an offence.

    → _____

13. They believe that there are no sea-serpents in Loch Ness.

    → _____

14. People fear that there will be a famine soon.

    → _____

PART 10

請用 "It is/was" 的型態將下列句子改寫為被動語態。

1. They assume that the answer is wrong.

   → _____

2. People claim that the country is neutral.

   → _____

3. They say that there is a way to make artificial grass.

   → _____

4. People said that she had nothing left to live for.

   → _____

5. They declared her the winner of the competition.

   → _____

6. They say that human beings are able to live on food capsules.

   → _____

7. People prophesy that there will be a Third World War.

   → _____

8. They no longer think that women have to stay at home.

   → _____

9. They believe that the house is haunted.

   → _____

10. We consider this dispute a matter of personal prejudice.

    → _____

11. They know that he is responsible for causing all the trouble.

    → _____

12. They assumed that there were no hitches in their plan.

    → _____

13. Some people believe that there is an afterworld.

    → _____

14. They claim that there is a nuclear center on the remote island.

    → _____

PART 11

請用被動語態改寫下列句子，不可使用 it 開頭。

1. People generally believe that money brings happiness.

    → _____

2. No one expects you to do it alone.

    → _____

3. They say that a cat has nine lives.

    → _____

4. They claimed that they were the winners.

    → _____

5. People consider the country the most developed in Asia.

    → _____

6. They fear that the boats are lost at sea.

    → _____

7. They understand that bribery is a crime.

    → _____

8. They consider him the best captain that they ever had.

    → _____

9. People no longer say that the moon is unconquerable.

    → _____

10. They considered the other method a better one.

    → _____

11. The ignorant natives believed that the white men had come from the moon.

    → _____

12. People knew that she was a dedicated social worker.

    → _____

13. They said that he was the most generous man in the village.

    → _____

14. People say that Shakespeare is the greatest poet of all time.

    → _____

15. They thought him to be a brilliant scientist.

→ _____

16. They believe her to be telling the truth.

→ _____

17. They assumed that he had eaten his dinner.

→ _____

18. People say that a bird in the hand is worth two in the bush.

→ _____

PART 12

請用被動語態改寫下列句子，不可使用 it 開頭。

1. People believe that the wishing well has magical powers.

→ _____

2. They claimed that the machine was able to do the work of twenty men.

→ _____

3. They say that the project has used up a large amount of money.

→ _____

4. People consider him the most eligible bachelor in town.

→ _____

5. People generally assume that money can buy most things.

→ _____

6. They suspect him to have taken part in the robbery.

→ _____

7. We believe that he was the sole heir to the large fortune.

→ _____

8. People say that smoking causes lung cancer.

→ _____

9. They assume that the telegram has reached the recipients.

→ _____

10. People consider the lion the king of the beasts.

→ _____

11. They understand that the examination is of vital importance to him.

→ _____

12. People believe he has some special knowledge which can help solve the case.

→ _____

13. They say that the rocket has circled four times around the moon.

→ _____

14. People fear that most of the houses have been washed away by the floodwaters.

→ _____

15. They believe that spirits of the dead are gathered in a place called "The Green Pastures."

→ _____

16. People think that this herb is a wonderful cure for coughs and colds.

→ _____

17. They assume that the temperature remains constant throughout the experiment.

→ _____

PART 13

請用 "It is/was" 的型態將下列句子改寫為被動語態。

1. They say that there is plenty of food in the oceans.

→ _____

2. They knew that there are no tigers in Africa.

→ _____

3. They supposed that the rats made those nests.

→ _____

4. They hope that all the races live in harmony together.

→ _____

5. They fear that there is a time bomb on the plane.

→ _____

6. People know that drastic changes have been made in the government.

→ _____

7. People no longer think that the world is flat.

→ _____

8. They consider this issue a matter of great importance.

→ _____

9. People fear that there will be a shortage of food in the near future.

→ _____

10. People generally assume that money is the root of all evil.

→ _____

11. They believe that he is guilty of the crime.

→ _____

12. They claim that there will be an earthquake in Tokyo this week.

→ _____

PART 14

請用被動語態改寫下列句子。

1. The bees attacked him when he accidentally disturbed their nest.

→ _____

2. Somebody has spilt ink all over the floor. Someone must wash the floor at once.

→ _____

3. They have made my father the secretary of the Rotary Club.

→ _____

4. Has someone paid the milkman yet?

→ _____

5. Somebody has broken the typewriter, and I can't use it anymore.

→ _____

6. They left the lighted candles and the flowers on the altar.

→ _____

7. Her unkind remarks about my paintings upset me very much.

→ _____

8. They pushed the car into the river so that no one would discover it.

→ _____

9. They believe that there will not be any changes in the timetable for the examination.

→ _____

10. The chairman is going to deliver a speech at the annual dinner.

→ _____

11. While they were showing her around the house, I went out into the garden.

→ _____

12. The villagers considered him to be an evil man.

→ _____

13. The director himself praised Mr. Baker for his thirty years of valuable service to the company.

→ _____

14. A poisonous type of spider makes this type of web.

→ _____

15. They will keep it as a secret if you pay them the money.

→ _____

16. An unknown poet wrote these words, and someone else set them to music.

→ _____

17. People blamed that girl for bringing bad luck to the village, and they chased her out of the district.

→ _____

18. The little boy's courage and determination impressed the lady very much.

→ _____

19. They had made the appointment before someone else invited them for dinner.

→ _____

20. The people in his hometown regarded him as a hero, and they welcomed him back with open arms.

→ _____

Chapter 12 語　氣

12-0 基本概念

語氣在條件句中可以用來表示「可能發生的事」（即直說語氣）和「不大可能或不可能發生的事」（即假設語氣）。

12-1 直說語氣

(a) 主要子句用未來式，而 if 引導的條件子句則用現在簡單式代替未來式。

USAGE PRACTICE

▶ If you **miss** the bus, you **will be** late for school.　如果你錯過這班公車，你上學將會遲到。

▶ If you **study** hard, you **will pass** the test easily.　如果你努力讀書，你將會輕鬆通過考試。

▶ If he **comes over**, I **will give** him the letter.　如果他過來，我將把這封信給他。

▶ She **will tell** me if I **ask** her.　如果我問她，她會告訴我。

▶ They **will be** offended if you **don't accept** their invitation.
　如果你不接受他們的邀請，他們會生氣。

▶ They **will fall** down if the branch **breaks**.　如果樹枝斷了，他們會摔下來。

▶ If it **rains**, we **will stay** at home.　如果下雨，我們將留在家裡。

 主要子句中的 will 可以用 can 或 may 代替。

▶ If you leave now, you **may** catch the train.　如果你現在離開，你可能還趕得上火車。

▶ He **can** go if he gets permission.　如果他獲得許可，他就能去。

▶ She **may** come along if she finishes the work.　如果她完成工作，她就可能會一起來。

▶ If she starts now, she **may** be in time.　如果她現在開始，她可能來得及。

(b) 當整個句子是一般的陳述，用來表達「自然的」或「被預期」之意的時候，主要子句和條件子句皆用現在簡單式。

USAGE PRACTICE

▶ If we **climb** higher, the air **gets** colder.　如果我們爬得越高，空氣就越冷。

▶ If I **am** hungry, I **eat** a sandwich.　如果我餓了，我就吃一個三明治。

▶ The ground **gets** wet if it **rains**. 如果下雨，地會變濕。

▶ If you **heat** wax, it **melts**. 如果你把蠟加熱，它會融化。

▶ If we **are** frightened, our hair **stands** on end. 如果我們害怕，毛髮會豎起來。

▶ A baby **cries** if it **is** hungry or in pain. 如果嬰兒餓了或痛了，就會哭。

▶ If it **is** summer in the Northern Hemisphere, it **is** winter in the Southern Hemisphere.
如果在北半球是夏天，在南半球就是冬天。

(c) 主要子句可以用祈使句。

USAGE PRACTICE

▶ If he asks for me, <u>**tell** him I'm not in</u>. 如果他要求見我，告訴他我不在。

▶ <u>**Try** again</u> if you fail in your first attempt. 如果你第一次嘗試失敗，再試一次。

(d) unless 也可以用來引導條件子句，相當於 if not，表示「除非」。

USAGE PRACTICE

▶ He won't work **unless** <u>you pay him well</u>. 除非你給他好的待遇，否則他不會做事。

▶ The plant won't live **unless** <u>you water it</u>. 除非你給植物澆水，否則它活不了。

▶ **Unless** <u>you go away at once</u>, I'll send for the police. 除非你立刻走開，否則我會叫警察。

▶ **Unless** <u>you hurry</u>, you will miss the bus. 除非你快一點，否則你會趕不上公車。

注意 條件子句也可以用 suppose (that)、on condition that、provided that 等連接詞來引導。

▶ **Suppose** the earth stops revolving, what will happen then?
如果地球停止運轉，到時將會發生什麼事呢？

▶ I will let you know the reason, **on condition that** you keep it confidential.
只要你保守祕密，我會讓你知道原因。

▶ **Provided that** you clean the lawnmower properly after use, you may borrow it.
假如你在使用割草機後會適當清理它，你就可以借用它。

 小練習

請根據提示在空格中填入正確的動詞型態，以完成直說語氣。

1. If there are no pineapples, she _____ (*buy*) some bananas instead.

2. He can have the shoes if they _____ (*be*) the right size for him.

3. If I _____ (*learn*) to smoke, my parents will be very displeased with me.

4. The wound _____ (*not heal*) unless you wash it and put some medicine on it.

5. If I give you the photographs, _____ you _____ (*promise*) not to show them to anyone?

6. A baby usually _____ (*cry*) if it _____ (*be*) tired or hungry.

7. If my guest comes over before I get home, please _____ (*entertain*) him for me.

8. He _____ (*play*) if you _____ (lend) him your tennis racket.

9. If we destroy their breeding places, the mosquitoes _____ (*not breed*) so easily.

10. Unless they agree to that condition, we _____ (*not accept*) them as members of our club.

11. He can reach the top shelf if he _____ (*stand*) on his toes.

12. If she goes out in the rain, she _____ (*catch*) a cold.

13. My mother _____ (*not feel*) happy unless I am home by that time.

14. If the weather is too hot, the crops _____ (*die*).

☞ 更多相關習題請見本章應用練習 Part 1 ～ Part 3。

12-2 假設語氣

(a) 表示「與現在事實相反」的假設語氣，條件子句用過去簡單式，而主要子句則用「should/would/could/might + 原形動詞」。

USAGE PRACTICE

▶ If I **had** a laptop, I **would send** this email myself.

如果我有筆記型電腦，我會自己寄這封電子郵件。

▶ I **would repair** it if I **knew** how to do it. 如果我知道怎麼修理它，我會把它修好。

▶ What **would** you **do** if you **lost** your way now? 假如你現在迷路了，你會怎麼做？

▶ You **would drown** if you **fell** into the pool. 如果你跌進水池，你會溺水。

▶ If you **spoke** too quickly, the children **would not understand** you.

如果你講得太快，孩子們會不明白你的意思。

▶ If we **had** the money, we **would buy** the boat now.

如果我們有錢，我們現在會買下那艘船。

基礎文法寶典 ❸
Essential English Usage & Grammar

(b) 條件子句的主詞不論其人稱為何或單複數，be 動詞都用 were，來表示「與現在事實相反」的假設語氣。

USAGE PRACTICE

▶ If I **were** the captain, I would not allow that to happen.

假如我是隊長，我不會准許那種事發生。

▶ If I **were** a bird, I would fly away to a warmer country.

假設我是一隻鳥，我會飛到比較溫暖的國家。

▶ If you **were** in my place, what would you do? 假使你處在我的立場，你會做什麼呢？

▶ He would be able to help us if he **were** here now. 假使他現在在這裡，他就能夠幫助我們。

▶ If she **were** my sister, I would lend her the money. 假如她是我的姊妹，我會把錢借給她。

▶ We would travel around the world if we **were** rich. 如果我們很富有，我們就會去環遊世界。

(c) 表示「與過去事實相反」的假設語氣，條件子句用過去完成式，而主要子句則用「should/would/could/might + have + 過去分詞」。

USAGE PRACTICE

▶ If I **had been** more careful, I **would not have caused** the accident.

假如我更小心些，我就不會造成這場意外了。

▶ I **would have bought** the LCD monitor if I **had had** the money.

如果我那時有錢，我就會買下那個液晶螢幕。

▶ I **could have found** your house if you **had given** me your address.

如果你當初給了我你的住址，我就可以找到你家。

▶ If you **had arrived** earlier, you **might have caught** the train.

如果你早一點到達，你就可能趕上火車。

▶ If he **had come** in time, he **would have met** her. 假如他及時來到，他就會遇見她。

▶ She **would have been** late for school if she **had missed** the bus.

如果她沒趕上公車，她上學就會遲到。

▶ If they **had told** us about their arrival, we **would have gone** to meet them.

如果他們當時跟我們說他們到達了，我們會去和他們會面。

▶ If they **had sent** the letter on Monday, we **could have received** it by Wednesday.

如果他們星期一就把信寄出，我們可能在星期三之前就可以收到它了。

▶ They **might have been** late if I **hadn't pointed** out the way to them.

如果我當時沒有為他們指路，他們可能會遲到。

▶ We **could have gotten** the rooms if we **had booked** them early.

假如我們早點預定，我們可能就有房間住。

▶ If the car **had crashed** into the lamppost, we **would have been killed**.

如果車子當時撞上街燈柱，我們就死定了。

(d) 表示「與未來事實相反」的假設語氣，條件子句用「were to + 原形動詞」或「should + 原形動詞」，其中 should 表示「萬一」；而主要子句則用「will/would/should/can/could/may/might + 原形動詞」。

USAGE PRACTICE

▶ If you **were to start** early tomorrow, you **wouldn't be** able to get there on time.

既使你明天提早出發，你也無法準時到達那裡。

▶ If there **should be** a typhoon tomorrow, what **can** we **do**?

萬一明天有颱風，我們能怎麼辦？

(e) 條件子句的 be 動詞或助動詞是 were、should 或 had 時，可以把 if 省略，把 were、should 或 had 置於句首，形成倒裝句。

USAGE PRACTICE

▶ If it **were** not for him, we would all have been killed.

→ **Were** it not for him, we would all have been killed.

如果不是他，我們早已全都被殺死了。

▶ If anyone **should** ask you about it, just say you don't know.

→ **Should** anyone ask you about it, just say you don't know.

萬一有任何人問你這件事，就說你不知道。

▶ If I **had known** he was such a trickster, I wouldn't have believed him.

→ **Had I known** he was such a trickster, I wouldn't have believed him.

如果我早知道他是一個這樣的騙子，我就不會相信他了。

基礎文法寶典❸
Essential English Usage & Grammar

請根據提示在空格中填入正確的動詞型態，以完成假設語氣。

1. _____ he _____ (*climb*) up onto the roof if I held the ladder for him?

2. She might be worried if he _____ (*not come*) home for dinner.

3. The branch _____ (*break*) if you clung to it.

4. If I _____ (*be*) a millionaire, I _____ (*build*) a home for the mentally challenged children in the town.

5. If you _____ (*be*) my father, I would not listen to your advice at all.

6. If they _____ (*catch*) up with him, they would give him a beating.

7. If he _____ (*go*) over now, he _____ (*find*) nobody in the house.

8. If he _____ (*make*) a slight mistake, he _____ (*lose*) his life.

9. Everybody _____ (*go*) home if a typhoon were coming.

10. He _____ (*withdraw*) his libel suit if Mr. Biggs _____ (*apologize*) to him publicly.

11. Even if I _____ (*be*) very poor, I _____ (*not accept*) any gifts or money from them.

12. He _____ (*agree*) to their proposal if they _____ (*allow*) him to have an equal share of the profits.

13. If she _____ (*break*) any of the apparatus, they _____ (*make*) her pay for them.

14. What would they do if they _____ (*send*) to the principal's office for breaking the school rules?

☞ 更多相關習題請見本章應用練習 Part 4 ～ Part 8。

Chapter 12　應用練習

PART 1

請根據提示在空格中填入正確的動詞型態，以完成直說語氣。

1. If she hears about it, there _____ (*be*) a lot of trouble for us.

2. If the sky _____ (*clear*) up soon, we will be able to go out.

3. They _____ (*not let*) you in if you don't give the password.

4. Unless you are a very good student, the college _____ (*not accept*) you.

5. If you climb higher, the air _____ (*become*) cooler.

6. _____ you _____ (*promise*) to keep it a secret if I tell you?

7. If she _____ (*come*) when I'm out, tell her to wait for me to return.

8. If the river _____ (*rise*) any higher, the town will be flooded.

9. Unless they _____ (*agree*) to his terms, he will refuse to sign the document.

10. If the water starts boiling, _____ (*switch*) off the electricity for me, please.

11. If it _____ (*continue*) raining, the river will overflow its banks.

12. I _____ (*not help*) you unless you tell me the whole truth.

13. Your body temperature _____ (*rise*) if you have a fever.

14. If the tunnels get blocked, what _____ (*happen*) to the miners?

15. If there are any letters for me, _____ (*bring*) them up, please.

16. Provided that you ask him politely, he _____ (*give*) you a reply.

17. They _____ (*not let*) you drive unless you have a license.

18. _____ (*not give*) up if you fail to achieve success the first time.

19. We _____ (*wait*) for you on condition that you come early.

20. Unless I see it for myself, I _____ (*not believe*) you.

21. Don't disturb the dog unless you _____ (*want*) to get bitten.

22. What will happen to the eggs if the mother bird _____ (*not return*) to its nest?

23. If the telephone rings, _____ (*not answer*) it.

24. If he is angry, he _____ (*keep*) a grim face.

PART 2

請根據提示在空格中填入正確的動詞型態,以完成直說語氣。

1. If you break the vase, you _____ (*get*) into trouble.

2. The glass _____ (*break*) if you plunge it into hot water.

3. I'm sure she _____ (*help*) us if we ask her nicely.

4. If I feel better, I _____ (*start*) work on it.

5. If we don't hurry, they _____ (*not wait*) for us.

6. If you take my advice, everything _____ (*be*) all right.

7. The bus _____ (*stop*) if you ring the bell.

8. We _____ (*meet*) you at the station if you come by train.

9. The dog _____ (*bark*) if it sees any strangers.

10. I'm sure she _____ (*remember*) if we leave the key on the table.

11. If he allows us to, we _____ (*go*) as soon as possible.

12. I _____ (*talk*) to her if I see her at the party.

13. If the phone rings, _____ you _____ (*take*) down the message for me?

14. The whole village _____ (*flood*) if the dam breaks.

15. I think they _____ (*sell*) you the car if you have five thousand dollars.

16. The grass soon _____ (*grow*) again if you don't cut the roots.

17. _____ you _____ (*believe*) me if I say that I've won first prize in the
lottery?

18. If you refuse to answer me, I _____ (*not let*) you go.

PART 3

請根據提示在空格中填入正確的動詞型態，以完成直説語氣。

1. Metals _____ (*expand*) if they are heated.

2. If it rains continuously for three days, the river _____ (*overflow*).

3. Ring the bell if you _____ (*want*) anything.

4. If lightning _____ (*strike*) this tree, we will all be killed.

5. If the telephone _____ (*ring*), don't answer it.

6. He _____ (*agree*) to the proposal if we discuss it with him.

7. If we _____ (*assist*) you in any way, do let us know.

8. What will happen if they _____ (*miss*) the only bus back to town?

9. We _____ (*be*) most grateful if you notify us.

10. Unless I _____ (*give*) you permission, you mustn't leave the room.

11. If we persuade her, she _____ (*change*) her mind.

12. If everyone _____ (*think*) about himself only, there will be havoc in the country.

13. What _____ (*happen*) if one supporting pillar is taken away?

14. If all of them _____ (*promise*) to do as I say, I will lead them across the marsh.

15. No one _____ ever _____ (*find*) out if we keep the secret to ourselves.

16. If the inspector comes around, _____ (*carry*) on as if there's nothing wrong.

17. She won't believe you unless she _____ (*see*) it for herself.

18. If you follow my instructions carefully, nothing _____ (*go*) wrong.

19. If you _____ (*wait*) awhile, I'll see what I can do.

20. She may change rooms if she _____ (*not like*) this one.

PART 4

請根據提示在空格中填入正確的動詞型態，以完成假設語氣。

1. They _____ (*be*) more pleased if you had told them the news yourself.

2. We could have given you our help if you _____ (*ask*) for it.

3. If she _____ (*not see*) the film, she would not have been able to tell us about it.

4. The whole field of corn _____ (*be*) on fire if you _____ (*burn*) the trash too close to it.

5. She _____ (*buy*) enough material for the curtains if she _____ (*measure*) the windows herself.

6. The clothes _____ (*dry*) if it hadn't been for the rain.

7. If I _____ (*have*) a cold, I would have stayed in bed.

8. If she _____ (*not give*) me those excuses, I _____ (*scold*) her.

9. The mosquitoes _____ (*bite*) you if you hadn't used mosquito coils.

10. If he _____ (*fall*) from the tree, he _____ (*break*) both legs.

11. She could have done better if you _____ (*give*) her more encouragement and help.

12. He might not have gotten ill if he _____ (*not eat*) those wild berries.

PART 5

請根據提示在空格中填入正確的動詞型態，以完成直說語氣或假設語氣。

1. You _____ (*hurt*) yourself if that branch broke.

2. If you aren't careful, you _____ (*spoil*) it.

3. If you worked out the sum carefully, you _____ (*get*) the answer easily.

4. The work will be finished more quickly if everyone _____ (*start*) working right now.

5. My brother _____ (*lend*) me the money if I asked him.

6. If I were Allen, I _____ (*report*) the incident to the police.

7. What _____ you _____ (*do*) even if you were there?

8. If you have enough common sense, you _____ (*realize*) that he needs your help.

9. What _____ you _____ (*tell*) her when she asks you?

10. If you _____ (*follow*) the instructions, you would not go wrong.

11. If she _____ (*be*) the teacher, she would forgive you.

12. We _____ (*not know*) the answer if we did not work it out.

13. I should be very happy if they _____ (*give*) me some sound advice.

14. It would be silly of you if you _____ (*not accept*) that invitation.

15. It would mean very much to him if you _____ (*drop*) in for a visit.

16. If you _____ (*be*) a bee, what flower would you visit most frequently?

17. If he were older, he _____ (*have*) more sense.

18. If the country _____ (*fail*) to produce enough food, many people would die of hunger.

19. If the drivers are more careful on the roads, there _____ (*be*) fewer accidents.

20. The team might win the match if they _____ (*practice*) hard enough.

21. The typhoon _____ (*damage*) many houses if it occurred here.

22. Ring the bell if you _____ (*require*) anything.

23. If I were a mouse, the cat _____ (*not catch*) me so easily.

24. The wet clothes will not dry if the sun _____ (*not shine*).

PART 6

請根據提示在空格中填入正確的動詞型態，以完成假設語氣。

1. If your message had not come, I _____ (*go*) off to my uncle's house.

2. If he _____ (*have*) a camera, he would have snapped a shot of the birds in flight.

3. The accident would never have happened if your brakes _____ (*be*) in perfect condition.

4. I wouldn't have been aware of it if it _____ (*not move*).

5. If the radio had not been on so loud, they _____ (*hear*) the knock at the door.

6. The robbers _____ (*not get*) away if the police had arrived on time.

7. The child might have drowned if that man _____ (*not jump*) in to rescue her.

8. The photograph would have been better if you _____ (*take*) it from this angle.

9. I _____ (*not lose*) my money if I had been more careful.

10. If the acrobat had lost his balance, he _____ (*drop*) from a height of thirty meters.

11. The animal _____ (*not escape*) if you had shut the gate properly.

12. If she _____ (*have*) time to think it over, she would not have agreed to their terms.

13. My mother would not have given me permission if she _____ (*know*) how dangerous it would be.

14. The flight _____ (*not delay*) if the weather had been fine.

15. The scouts might have found their way out if they _____ (*bring*) a compass with them.

16. Suppose I had given a negative answer—what _____ you _____ (*do*)?

17. If you _____ (*work*) harder, you might have passed your examination.

18. _____ you _____ (*rescue*) her if she had been your enemy?

PART 7

請根據提示在空格中填入正確的動詞時態，以完成直說語氣或假設語氣。

1. If you listen carefully to the tape, you _____ (*hear*) the sound of a child crying.

2. If I _____ (*see*) a tiger, I would run for my life.

3. If he _____ (*spray*) insecticide on the plant, all the ants would die.

4. We _____ (*play*) football on the field if it doesn't rain.

5. You will strain yourself if you _____ (*try*) to lift that box all by yourself.

6. I _____ (*show*) you how to operate that machine if you were willing to learn.

7. If I _____ (*be*) your mother, I would not let you go.

8. Many people _____ (*injure*) if the stage collapses.

9. If he _____ (*pull*) out the plug while the current was on, he would get an electric shock.

10. Those trees _____ (*bear*) fruit earlier if you planted them from grafts.

11. _____ you _____ (*buy*) the shares if the price had been lower?

12. The man _____ (*not sell*) you that medicine unless you have a prescription from your doctor.

13. If there _____ (*not be*) so much publicity about the show, it would not have been so successful.

14. If you _____ (*drive*) carefully around the bend, there wouldn't have been an accident.

15. _____ she _____ (*wade*) across the river if the bridge had collapsed?

16. She _____ (*start*) cooking if she has all the ingredients ready.

PART 8

請根據提示在空格中填入正確的動詞時態，以完成直說語氣或假設語氣。

1. If we hadn't gotten your message, we _____ (*go*) without you.

2. If she _____ (*realize*) that her father was so ill, she would have stayed on to take care of him.

3. You will be able to travel with them if there _____ (*be*) space for you in their car.

4. He _____ (*deliver*) the goods to your house if he had the time.

5. If it were not for her, my father _____ (*not know*) about the incident.

6. If you painted the wall a different color, it _____ (*make*) a great difference to the room.

7. If someone gave you a million dollars, what _____ you _____ (*do*) with it?

8. If he had consulted a doctor earlier, he _____ (*recover*) by now.

9. If you require anything else, just _____ (*call*) me.

10. If we find there is truth in what he says, then we _____ (*believe*) him.

11. Christopher _____ (*not tell*) us his plan unless we tell him about ours first.

12. The children _____ (*allow*) to go to their aunt's house on condition that you accompanied them.

13. The plane may be diverted to Singapore if the bad weather _____ (*continue*).

14. The clock might have stopped if you _____ (*not wind*) it the night before.

15. If I _____ (*be*) your brother, I would accept the invitation.

16. He might have time to see her if she _____ (*be*) to go to his office.

17. I _____ (*answer*) the phone if I hadn't been taking my bath at that time.

18. If there are any letters for me, just _____ (*keep*) them with you.

19. I _____ (*not suspect*) her if she hadn't spoken to me about it.

20. He _____ (*not call*) the doctor unless it were something serious.

基礎文法寶典❸
Essential English Usage & Grammar
習題解答

Chapter 10 解答

10–1 小練習

1. changes　　2. wakes　　3. doesn't rain　　4. play; don't play　　5. Do; smoke; don't　　6. takes

7. puts　　8. opens　　9. meets; is　　10. provide; serve　　11. is; revolves; rotates

12. cleans; doesn't clean　　13. live; walk; don't mind; ask

10–2 小練習

1. was　　2. woke; prepared　　3. was; had　　4. lent　　5. used; was　　6. wore　　7. boiled; made

8. didn't break; broke　　9. didn't have; left　　10. was; saw　　11. thought; was; told

12. shouted; needed　　13. took; glanced; gave　　14. replied; was; planned

15. saw; skidded; bumped; smashed

10–3 小練習

1. will polish　　2. will refuse　　3. won't disappoint; will　　4. will be　　5. will celebrate

6. Will; go; will be　　7. won't clear　　8. will last　　9. will play　　10. Will; buy　　11. won't be

12. will; meet　　13. Won't; listen

10–4 小練習

1. are sorting　　2. is painting　　3. am helping; Are; coming　　4. are unloading

5. is washing; isn't ironing　　6. are packing; are leaving　　7. are sleeping

8. Are; whistling; am working　　9. is making; is speaking　　10. is leaving; are traveling

11. are learning; are putting; is turning　　12. is coming; is stopping; are gathering

13. is telling; isn't repairing; is going　　14. Are; paying; am giving

10–5 小練習

1. was; doing　　2. was baking　　3. was doing　　4. was dancing; was playing　　5. was strolling

6. were standing　　7. was searching　　8. were following　　9. was eating; was playing

10. was getting; was wearing　　11. was listening; was watching　　12. was shopping; was sitting

13. were; talking; were discussing　　14. was; doing; was looking; was making

10–6 小練習

1. will be aching　　2. will be appearing　　3. will; be burning　　4. will be carrying; Will; be taking

5. won't be entertaining; will be camping　　6. will be finishing　　7. will be celebrating

8. will be preparing　　9. will be wearing　　10. will be waking

11. will be paying; Will; be accompanying　　12. will; be raining　　13. will be traveling; will be dreaming

14. will be departing; will be seeing   15. will be going; won't be coming

10–7 小練習

1. has happened; Has; hurt   2. Have; told   3. have; sent   4. hasn't eaten

5. has; made; Has; heard   6. has been; hasn't started; has forgotten   7. has bought   8. have had

9. has torn; has scratched   10. has washed; has put; Have; seen   11. has won; Have; heard; has been

10–8 小練習

1. had; seen   2. had been   3. had taken   4. had broken   5. had employed   6. Had; happened

7. had memorized   8. had taken   9. had been   10. had known   11. had learned   12. had gone

13. had hammered

10–9 小練習

1. will have reached   2. will have informed   3. will have traveled   4. will have been

5. will have seen   6. will have come   7. will have found   8. will have burned

9. will have switched   10. will have persuaded   11. will have climbed   12. will have heard

13. will have moved   14. will have sailed   15. will have used   16. will have graduated

17. will have learned   18. will have written   19. will have eaten   20. will have spread

21. will have worked   22. will have seen

10–10 小練習

1. has been ringing   2. haven't been writing   3. has been waiting   4. has been calling

5. has been studying   6. have been trying   7. have; been sitting   8. Have; been behaving

9. have been bullying   10. have been looking; have; been doing

11. has been boiling; Haven't; been waiting

10–11 小練習

1. had been borrowing   2. had been lying   3. had; been hiding   4. had been leaking

5. had been ringing   6. had been counting   7. had been raining   8. had been working

9. had been going   10. hadn't been listening   11. had been waiting   12. had been watching

13. had been climbing   14. had been doing   15. had been bathing   16. had been running

應用練習

PART 1

1. gives; kills   2. obeys; says   3. travels   4. hurries; tell; is; listens   5. reaches

6. doesn't work; goes   7. sets   8. are cleaned; does   9. depends; agrees   10. works; brings

11. doesn't break; is   12. seems; is   13. rises; comes; bows   14. Do; know; live   15. spend; does

16. leaves; doesn't wait   17. swings; sends; gives; lands

PART 2

1. gets   2. doesn't matter; goes   3. is   4. leaves   5. rises; sets   6. does; studies; is

7. comes; Doesn't; look   8. goes; return   9. crows; is   10. believes; says   11. is; knows

12. leaves; reaches   13. studies; hopes; knows; get   14. doesn't stop; sails; reaches

15. gets; jumps; claps   16. is; misplaces; finds; gets; turns

PART 3

1. rotates; revolves   2. reach; send   3. leaves; arrives

4. passes; rushes; intercepts; throws; dashes; grabs   5. selects; carves; resembles; polishes; is

6. flows; meanders   7. plays; doesn't come; returns; takes; changes

8. delivers; brings; are; comes; leaves   9. leaves; reaches; don't hurry

10. comes; inquires; tell; am; don't want   11. know; take; learn   12. dislikes; gives; prefers

13. fasten; wait; leaves; rises   14. collects; measures; needs; begins; works; is

15. swings; dodges; seizes; delivers   16. stop; move; visit; set

PART 4

1. sleeps; is; works   2. travels; sends; goes   3. start; end   4. shows; marks   5. seem; looks

6. get; rises   7. branches; follows   8. reminds; works   9. come   10. says; cost   11. build; rains

12. clean; needs   13. flows; passes; reaches   14. crack; are   15. marks; comes   16. reaches; is

17. burns; lasts   18. expects; recommends; don't intend   19. thinks; knows; finds

20. forks; leads; takes

PART 5

1. marched; reached; had; continued   2. dived; swam   3. removed; hung; sat; began

4. celebrated; was; lasted   5. started; walked; rushed   6. studied; did   7. walked; seemed; rang

8. tripped; fell; hurried   9. leaped; was   10. lived; used   11. spent; was; bought; visited

12. came; had; ate; went   13. thrilled; clapped; cheered; scored   14. didn't talk; was   15. tasted; began

16. didn't understand; found   17. Did; suffer; died; was   18. Did; carry; tipped

19. told; went; didn't enjoy; wished   20. ran; opened; went   21. Were; failed; wasn't   22. came; caught

23. broke; stole; discovered   24. felt; rushed; treated

PART 6

1. took; tore; began   2. wrote; sealed   3. stepped; skidded; collided   4. practiced; was

5. saw; passed   6. didn't turn; didn't want   7. swung; shook   8. bored; escaped

9. tidied; swept; went   10. remembered; came   11. tried; kicked   12. laughed; ached

13. took; washed   14. Did; sleep; inquired   15. became; sank   16. flickered; whispered

17. traveled; reached   18. started; discovered

PART 7

1. will be   2. will cook   3. won't forget   4. Will; go   5. will stay   6. will ring; Will; line

7. will write   8. will; plant   9. will help   10. will leave; will do   11. will; get   12. Won't; wipe

13. will contribute   14. will take; will be   15. will leave; will miss   16. will be served; will be

PART 8

1. will meet   2. Will; push   3. will ring   4. will go; will be   5. will ask; will be

6. will succeed   7. won't vote   8. will have; Will; join   9. will; see

10. won't forgive   11. will arrive; Will; go   12. will; spend; will let

13. will start; won't pass; will have

PART 9

1. We are going to cook dinner tonight.   2. I am not going to sit for the piano examination this year. 3. He is going to get you a ticket for the concert.   4. Your uncle is certainly going to give you a good birthday present.   5. The whole family is going to shift to the new house next month.   6. She is going to attend the wedding lunch on his behalf.   7. The mayor is going to deliver the speech.   8. They are going to leave for Greensville in a few days. They are not going to return to Fairtown for his wedding. 9. I am not going to encourage him to eat cakes or candy. They spoil his appetite.   10. Are you ready? We are not going to wait for you any longer.   11. I am going to play tennis with her this evening. Are you going to be the referee?   12. Are you going to fetch your shoes from the cobbler this afternoon? 13. Are we going to have a swim before we go back to the chalet?   14. It is not going to rain. The wind is going to blow those dark clouds away.

PART 10

1. will travel   2. will listen   3. will rain; will; bring   4. will drive   5. won't do   6. will fly

7. will; invite   8. will; end; will be   9. will; tell   10. will allow   11. will take   12. will go

13. will demonstrate

PART 11

1. will shut; will rain   2. will help; will come   3. will come   4. won't believe; will convince

5. will ask; will take   6. will know; won't leave   7. will need; Shall; get   8. Will; throw; will fetch

9. will land; Shall; go   10. won't open   11. will leave   12. will; come; won't wait

13. will; do; Will; be   14. will spend; won't set   15. will see; will tell

PART 12

1. is making   2. is getting   3. are going; Are; coming   4. is; making   5. is ringing; are lining

6. are; going; am going   7. are suffering; is doing   8. is boiling; Aren't; going

9. is making; is preparing; is giving   10. is walking; is turning; looking; is waving

PART 13

1. are having; is boiling   2. is spreading; are taking   3. is looking   4. is waiting; Is; going

5. is drooping; are looking   6. are growing; are expecting   7. is baking; is sifting

8. Is; laughing; Isn't; doing   9. is using; is cutting   10. is greasing; is checking

11. is cleaning; is watering   12. are moving; am helping   13. is cooking; listening

14. is working; is taking   15. am not expecting; am wondering   16. is selecting; is hoping

PART 14

1. is shutting; wants; is   2. like; are reading   3. don't wear; am wearing; is   4. interferes; are doing

5. are attending; starts   6. Are; is congratulating; are expecting   7. drives; is taking; is

8. is knocking; is walking; is; are going   9. talks; isn't talking; is suffering; is; isn't eating

PART 15

1. is opening   2. is getting; doesn't want; says; doesn't have   3. does; are dressing

4. comes; is helping   5. am speaking; come; is raining   6. have; am staying

7. Is; coming; tell; don't have   8. have; sells; is; are taking   9. consists; do; understand; am taking

10. is; likes; are listening; Do; understand   11. don't like; are giving

PART 16

1. am going; think; wants   2. is burning; wonder; is   3. is; is feeling   4. is waiting; says; wants

5. am leaving; leaves   6. are; shivering; Are; feeling; am   7. are discussing; thinks; has

8. are having; Do; know; are talking   9. doesn't like; is; isn't leaving   10. is; is; understands; says

11. has; is; needs; is coming   12. wonder; is barking; hear; is coming

13. Does; belong; doesn't; belongs; brings   14. am trying; is having; is singing

15. loses; does; screams; Do; hear; is yelling

PART 17

1. is; practice; have; are playing; is raining   2. is showing; wants; tell; starts

3. is; is blowing; are swaying; are flying; think   4. is; is sitting; is dancing; enjoying

5. have; contains; need; am sewing; hope; likes   6. are going; want; am making; need; isn't; buy

7. likes; is; takes; reads; is studying   8. are staging; are doing; are coming

9. is; am going; is traveling; Are; coming   10. are flying; buy; make   11. sweeps; dusts; grumbles; has

12. are; takes; exchanges; is planting; says   13. have; am not going; feel; want

14. comes; asks; am; am waiting; have; hope; likes

15. walk; gaze; hear; are breaking; are crawling; are trying   16. take; is repainting; dries

17. are cleaning; are taking; dusting   18. is coming; are running; shouting; waving; have

19. is; are putting; are watching; are trying

PART 18

1. are having; wonder; are talking   2. is discussing; have   3. listens; says; is; thinking

4. are organizing; has   5. travels; is traveling; enjoys; feels; sleeps

6. says; is coming; is sailing; makes   7. am writing; want; miss   8. go; is coming; is; shut

9. Do; see; is climbing; reaches; picks; drops   10. is ringing; is answering; is

11. is making; tastes; looks   12. hates; is having; call; refuses   13. grumbles; rains; shines; seems

14. are; waiting; are; know; want; are having

PART 19

1. are working; is   2. is crowing; think; is   3. are flying; are eating   4. are going; hope

5. is raining; believe   6. is; nagging; think; doesn't seem

7. feeds; am doing; has   8. is lying; is sleeping   9. doesn't matter; bring

10. is getting; is disappearing   11. are going; is staying; has   12. boasts; is; telling

13. is having; is singing   14. recognizes; is barking; wagging   15. Do; understand; is saying; seems

16. Are; having; are; discussing   17. contains; Do; smell   18. knows; are; coming

19. doesn't want; prefers; is watching   20. is; talking; wish; am

PART 20

1. were talking   2. were standing; were chatting   3. was crying; was preparing   4. was; sewing

5. was finishing; was; beginning   6. were; complaining   7. was; working

8. were swimming; was sunbathing   9. was watering; was cooking   10. weren't listening; was talking

11. was reading; were doing   12. was passing   13. were setting; were cooking

14. were running   15. was searching; was grumbling   16. were barking; was limping

PART 21

1. was wearing   2. was redecorating   3. was running

4. were shouting; fighting; was trying   5. was having; was sewing   6. was learning

7. were collecting   8. was; burning   9. were crawling; was trying   10. was preparing; was mowing

11. was walking   12. was; finding   13. was; hoping   14. was listening; was reading

15. were; doing; Were; practicing; was studying

PART 22

1. was getting; realized   2. was holding; was; blew   3. knew; was happening; went

4. was hiding; were searching   5. was standing; invited; brought   6. were walking; began; ran

7. was explaining; stood; asked   8. was raining; sat   9. fell; knew; was happening; was

10. arrived; were; standing   11. were; grumbling; were; realized   12. thought; was; tried; found; was

13. was sleeping; broke; were; rescued   14. was waiting; was getting; was running; got; drove

PART 23

1. was cleaning; went; killed   2. stopped; was speeding   3. came; was discussing; broke; invited

4. was playing; were dancing; were dining   5. spent; had; knew

6. was searching; saw; was talking; waving   7. was opening; heard; paused; listened; were coming

8. was driving; noticed; were sailing   9. arrived; was waiting

10. was; complaining; said; didn't like; was trying   11. was walking; didn't know; was coming; hit

12. was staying; accompanied   13. were driving; stopped; told; was looking; ordered

14. was dressing; called; was rushing; tripped; fell   15. was raining; were waiting; streaked; rumbled

PART 24

1. entered; was talking   2. was cooking; started   3. fell; was running; was; crying; reached

4. were fighting; escaped   5. were looking; was sleeping   6. was walking; stepped; fell

7. carried; was raining; saw; shut; ran   8. was reading; went; didn't come

9. did; interrupt; were having   10. seemed; saw   11. were searching; found   12. was cycling; started

13. was having; rang; was cooking; had   14. was watering; stung; swelled   15. were; arguing; arrived

16. was driving; stopped; asked   17. was listening; heard; opened; saw

PART 25

1. was taking; heard; was; ran; brought   2. was; reading; went   3. was painting; knocked

4. reminded; didn't listen   5. woke; told; was trying   6. saw; was hurrying   7. waved; was; saw

8. didn't recognize; started   9. weren't working; didn't know   10. was carrying; slipped

11. were writing; stopped   12. was; lying; opened; was   13. were eating; went; offered; didn't take

PART 26

1. was raining; reached   2. started; were getting   3. reached; found   4. was studying; rang

5. were discussing; came   6. were shouting; left   7. took; weren't looking

8. were going; skidded; landed   9. was writing; heard; opened; found

10. saw; was trimming; was talking; cut   11. was carrying; tripped; fell; ran; managed

12. was pressing; heard; were coming   13. went; was preparing; asked; agreed

PART 27

1. will; be having   2. won't be coming   3. will be passing   4. will be spending

5. will; be raining   6. will be coming   7. will be lecturing   8. will not be sailing

9. will be driving   10. won't be making; will be attending   11. won't be staying

12. will be putting; Will; be participating   13. will; be weeding   14. will be having

15. will be observing   16. won't be leaving   17. will be listening; watching

18. will be teaching; will be taking   19. will be leaving; will be looking

20. will be sleeping; will be waiting

PART 28

1. will; be cooking   2. will be taking   3. will be traveling   4. will be flying   5. will be raining

6. will be coming   7. will; be doing; Will; be working   8. will be going   9. will be looking

10. will be arriving; will be sleeping   11. will be working; will be having   12. will be watching

13. will be waiting   14. will be walking   15. will be taking; will be telling

16. will be waiting; will be wagging; barking   17. will be coming; will be sailing

18. will; be living; will be having

PART 29

1. will be sweeping   2. will be visiting   3. will be sitting   4. will be working   5. will be leaving

6. will be gasping   7. will be watching   8. Will; be bringing   9. will be blooming

10. will be coming   11. will be preparing   12. will; be raining

13. will be cleaning; will; be doing; will be catching

PART 30

1. will assemble   2. will be flying   3. will do; will be praying   4. Will; put   5. will be walking

6. will take   7. will be starting   8. won't help   9. won't be coming   10. won't be acting; will have

11. won't open   12. will be pulling   13. will be waiting; Will; finish

14. will be celebrating; will buy; will decorate   15. will be looking   16. won't be; will be attending

17. will be playing; Will; ask   18. will be seeing

PART 31

1. have just had   2. have already received; haven't carried   3. have often helped; has often taught

4. Has; ever shown   5. have seldom spoken   6. have never been   7. has never happened

8. have spoiled   9. have just decided   10. has recently completed   11. Has; ever confided

12. has just made   13. has taken almost   14. have nearly finished; have just mopped

15. have never been; have completely forgotten   16. have just heard; Have; heard

17. has often won; Have; ever been   18. have always tried; have always refused

PART 32

1. has asked   2. Has; arrived   3. has done   4. has dropped   5. have; told   6. Has; swept

7. have asked; has refused   8. Have; thought; have taken   9. has; forgotten; have reminded

10. have invited; have prepared   11. has taught; have; liked   12. have; paid; haven't got

13. has; left; hasn't arrived   14. has been; has taken   15. has; left; has gone; haven't seen

16. Have; seen; have lost   17. has; returned; has brought; has; had   18. Has; told

PART 33

1. have; borrowed; Have; read   2. have bought; have finished   3. has heard; Have; heard

4. has treated; assured   5. has worked; has become   6. has used   7. has returned; has; eaten

8. have fed; haven't fed; haven't prepared   9. has fought; has broken   10. has sown

11. haven't made; have; done   12. has rung; haven't come   13. has; decided; hasn't been

14. Have; thought; have had   15. has behaved; hasn't cried; has eaten   16. has worked; has saved

PART 34

1. has left; has pinned   2. has broken   3. has fallen; has dived   4. Have; decided; have given

5. haven't seen; Has; been   6. have read; haven't reached; have had   7. have; been; have; done

8. have asked   9. has returned; hasn't brought   10. hasn't rained; has; dried

11. Has; written; have; received   12. have been   13. has; explained; has; finished

14. haven't gone; have; planned   15. Have; found   16. have thought; have; decided

PART 35

1. has gone; bought; had   2. has; signed; Has; asked   3. hasn't arrived; received   4. was; has left

5. has fallen; has; come; examined   6. has; healed; has; been; hurt   7. Have; been; went; enjoyed

8. asked; haven't done   9. inherited; has used   10. has taught; has passed   11. wound; has stopped

12. has; swum; Did; swim

PART 36

1. has found; was   2. hasn't set; didn't put   3. kneeled; began   4. Have; ridden; haven't tried

5. has just been; left　6. wanted; didn't have　7. has been; came　8. have never seen

9. hasn't finished; Did; watch; Did; make　10. has; been; joined; has; become　11. locked; drove

12. has taken; left; has disappeared　13. advised; left; went; ate

PART 37

1. haven't seen; heard; has gone　2. have emailed; sent　3. left; have asked　4. came; hasn't got

5. has adopted; saw　6. has delivered; ordered; Have; paid　7. arrived; has visited

8. has invited; have prepared　9. gave; have named　10. have seen; saw; said

11. has known; have lived　12. found; wanted; started　13. Have; been; have been

14. was; has washed　15. found; Did; lose; were　16. gave; took　17. promised; finished

PART 38

1. have known; was; has changed　2. was; has promised　3. have/did; put; have searched

4. has; finished; took; did　5. have; finished; started; have made　6. have found; lost; picked

7. has gone　8. started; have; finished　9. wrote; asked　10. told; have ignored/ignored

11. were; waited; left　12. have; waited; told; was; came; was

13. caught; looked; gave; named; adopted

PART 39

1. Have; seen; have promised　2. haven't seen; wanted　3. told; has; returned

4. bought; used; took　5. haven't seen; have dropped; did; use　6. has worked; has; thought; has said

7. occurred; damaged; have reported　8. have; received; haven't paid; have mad; paid

9. applied; haven't received　10. told; has lived; has; been　11. has; decided; was; was; wanted

12. weeded; have grown　13. told; have arrived; Have; been　14. said; have had; has happened

15. haven't seen, told; went; Has; come　16. has gone; has; been; was

17. Have; understood; have prepared

PART 40

1. haven't visited; wanted　2. have found; lost; have left　3. haven't seen; has wandered

4. have known; haven't seen　5. has; returned; visited　6. has gone; have; been; was

7. haven't seen; Has; returned; called; answered　8. has left; slipped; had

9. tried; believed; was; refused　10. have; agreed; didn't want; explained

11. borrowed; haven't returned; haven't finished　12. has been; hasn't sent; promised; arrived

13. got; has seized　14. took; have left; has stopped　15. broke; reported; has come

16. have; wanted; have had　17. saw; haven't seen, enjoyed

PART 41

1. had happened   2. had dug   3. had had   4. had taken   5. had; gone   6. had delayed

7. had hidden   8. had opened; had flown   9. had finished   10. had shut; had locked

11. had happened; had heard; received   12. had been; had slept

PART 42

1. had done   2. had started   3. had upset   4. had fought   5. hadn't told; had kept

6. had rung; hadn't arrived   7. had stopped   8. hadn't seen   9. had been; had visited

10. had finished   11. had expected; had behaved   12. had submitted; hadn't been

13. had hoped; had waited

PART 43

1. had written; went   2. arrived; had already died   3. told; had left   4. had finished; went

5. had given; realized   6. reached; had left   7. said; had lost   8. had swept; asked

9. locked; had put   10. had started   11. had tied; threw   12. had got; stopped   13. left; had given

PART 44

1. had; rung; reached   2. was; hadn't seen; looked   3. said; had; seen; knew

4. proved; had thought   5. Had; finished; began   6. had been   7. had had; packed; called

8. walked; had chosen; paid   9. had run; came; rested   10. remembered; hadn't turned; was

11. came; knew; had happened   12. told; had broken; was; had escaped

13. had promised; came; was; had lent   14. trusted; let; was; refused

15. replied; never received; was; had written; hadn't replied

PART 45

1. wound; had stopped   2. had tarred; started   3. searched; remembered; had left

4. proved; had thought   5. had; seen; recognized; had described   6. were; had failed

7. had had; went   8. were; came   9. caught; had; had handcuffed; had taken   10. had dusted; swept

11. had; gone; heard; came; ran; had stopped   12. left; had

13. had hung; started; began; had collected; stopped   14. were; reached   15. heard; ran; had happened

16. didn't know; had come; reached

PART 46

1. will have closed   2. will have finished   3. will have gone   4. Will; have had

5. will have gone   6. will; have finished   7. will have got

8. will; have finished   9. will have repaired   10. will have had   11. will have painted

12. will have read   13. will have changed; will have grown; will have changed

PART 47

1. will have lived   2. will have gone   3. will have heard   4. will have left   5. will have repaired

6. will have understood   7. will have started   8. will have set   9. will have learned

10. will have persuaded   11. will have been   12. will have known

PART 48

1. have been living   2. has been practicing   3. have been trying   4. has been playing

5. have; been doing; Have; been painting   6. have been polishing   7. has been barking

8. have been studying   9. have been staring; have been trying

10. haven't been sleeping; have; Have; been working   11. has; been using; have been waiting

12. have been trying; has; been lying   13. has been shopping   14. have been driving; have been sitting

15. has been watering; have been weeding   16. have been working; Have; been helping

PART 49

1. has been paying   2. has been doing; haven't been idling   3. has been playing

4. has been working; has been sleeping   5. has been resting; has been reading

6. have been rearranging; has been helping   7. hasn't been feeling; hasn't been attending

8. has been baking   9. have been investigating   10. hasn't been taking; has been wearing

11. Have; been watching; have been studying   12. have been working

PART 50

1. has been working; for   2. have; been studying; Have; been taking; since

3. has been sewing; since   4. has been crying; for   5. has been raining; since

6. has been lying; for   7. have been walking; for   8. has been teaching; since

9. has been boiling; for   10. have been listening; for   11. has been wearing; since

12. has been eating; for   13. have; been doing; since   14. have been playing; since

15. have been studying; for   16. has been coughing; since   17. has been standing; since

18. have been using; for

PART 51

1. have eaten; have set   2. has been attending   3. has completed   4. has been; has come

5. haven't succeeded; has been snoring   6. have been trying.   7. has been waiting

8. has been blowing; have gathered   9. has caught; has been staying

10. have come; have been unloading   11. haven't paid; haven't been sleeping; have been feeling

12. have offered; Have; been following   13. has been watching; have reported; have been doing

14. has been digging; has just heard

PART 52

1. has been crying; have disturbed   2. have been sitting; Have; had

3. have been waiting; has forgotten   4. have been avoiding; have happened

5. have; been; have been looking   6. has been going; has lost

7. have been shouting; yelling; have found; has taken   8. has been working

9. has been sitting; have called; hasn't taken

10. have; been doing; have cooked; have been; has been tempting   11. have heard; has; recovered

PART 53

1. have been waiting; hasn't turned   2. have been looking; haven't seen

3. has been reading; has neglected   4. have heard; have; met   5. have been standing; haven't noticed

6. have been whispering; have been watching   7. have had   8. has lost; has been trying; has had

9. has been smoking; has; left   10. has been lying; Have; checked   11. has come; has been visiting

12. have been walking; haven't seen   13. has been sewing; have; spent

14. has been playing; have heard   15. has been reading; has taken   16. has given; have been waiting

PART 54

1. has been discussing; haven't reached   2. has been working; has; met

3. has been thinking; hasn't made   4. has been learning; hasn't put; has learned

5. haven't seen; have; been doing   6. hasn't been; has happened   7. have been looking; haven't been

8. have been fishing; haven't had   9. has been practicing; has interrupted

10. have known; have; visited   11. has been hanging; hasn't broken; has shown

12. have been concentrating; have neglected

PART 55

1. has been thinking; hasn't thought   2. have been fishing; haven't caught

3. have; disliked; have been trying   4. has been eating; has eaten

5. haven't understood; have been sleeping   6. have been working; haven't seen

7. hasn't rained; has dried   8. have been observing; have noticed   9. has been watching; hasn't had

PART 56

1. has been saving; has saved   2. has been mewing; Have; fed   3. has been leaking; haven't called

4. has been standing; has decided   5. hasn't bought; has been

6. have been building; haven't completed   7. have been studying; haven't obtained   8. hasn't had

9. Has; forgotten; have been reminding; has been

PART 57

1. had been crying   2. had been hiking   3. had been fishing   4. had been staring

5. had been working   6. Had; been writing   7. had been building   8. had been sitting

9. had been doing   10. had been helping   11. had been using   12. had been studying

PART 58

1. hadn't been paying   2. had; been telling   3. had been knocking   4. Had; been playing

5. hadn't been reading; had been sleeping   6. hadn't been talking   7. hadn't been taking

8. hadn't been thinking   9. had been pestering   10. had been spreading   11. had been eating

12. Had; been supporting

PART 59

1. had been ringing   2. had been looking   3. Had; been scolding   4. had been splashing

5. had; been talking   6. had been teaching   7. had been driving   8. had been searching

9. had been writing   10. had been meddling   11. had been staying   12. had been painting

Chapter 11 解答

11–1 小練習

1. is being repaired; is spoiled   2. is not being used; is being repaired

3. is expected; are being announced   4. are told; are being considered   5. is given; is being read

6. are being taken; are peeled; washed; cooked; canned   7. are taken; are; left

8. are warned; is printed; is being broadcast   9. are not being used; are spoiled; are kept

10. are being loaded; is exported   11. is grown; is exported; are being taken

12. are being washed; is put   13. is produced; is being shown   14. is being kept; is feared

15. are stationed; is being searched   16. is being cleaned; is allowed

17. are made; are assembled; are being made   18. is hoped; are being taken

19. are being sold; is being built

11–2 小練習

1. The cookies are baked over a charcoal fire.   2. The minutes of the meeting will be written by the secretary.   3. The problem has been discussed for several days.   4. The radio has been switched on.

5. That block of flats was built in 1973.   6. Our team was beaten in the hockey match yesterday.   7.

Flies are often found near rubbish dumps.　8. Our house was broken into last night.　9. The poem, "The Pied Piper of Hamelin," was written by Robert Browning.　10. "Were you told where to report for work?" "No, I was not told."　11. Many buildings were destroyed and many people were killed by the earthquake.　12. Many types of seashells can be found along the seashore. This place is visited by many people during the school holidays.　13. Iron ore has been discovered on the tiny island. An expert has been sent there to investigate.　14. The skins of the potatoes should be peeled before they are cooked.

11–3 小練習

1. I was told a very sad story about her.　2. I was given the wrong change at the shop.　3. Women in most countries have been given the right to vote.　4. A set of silver cutlery will be given to them on their silver wedding anniversary.　5. He has been promised a reward if he finds the dog.　6. The lecturer was asked a very difficult question.　7. He will not be told the truth about the situation.　8. A job was offered to him, but it was turned down.　9. A second serving of ice cream is being given to each child.　10. An autograph book was given to him to sign.

11–4 小練習

1. The child will be taken care of properly.　2. Research is being conducted into the private life of that great sculptor.　3. These problems will be dealt with one at a time.　4. The old notice was taken down, and another one was put up in its place.　5. Tom was ordered out of the classroom by the teacher because too much noise was being made by him.　6. The hall lights were left on in case they decided to come back that night.　7. The detective was locked in while he was absorbed in examining something.　8. The landmarks of the town were pointed out to me by my uncle.　9. When they were halfway there, they suddenly realized that Emily had been left behind.　10. All my washing has been messed up by the little boys who were playing in the garden this morning.

11–5 小練習

1. He is considered to be the richest man in the country.　2. These herbs are said to be good for rheumatism.　3. She is thought to be the most understanding and patient teacher in the school.　4. The boy was thought to be joking when he mentioned his part in the tragedy.　5. Witches from nearby villages were believed to meet in the woods when the moon was full.　6. He was said to marry his wife while he was abroad.　7. He is known to be a wanted man.　8. Blood is said to be always thicker than water.　9. He was believed to be the strongest man living.　10. The product was claimed to be the best on the market.　11. The Vikings are said to have discovered America first.　12. Fat people are generally assumed to be lazy.　13. He was seen to be committing the crime.　14. She was seen to take a letter out

of the letter box.   15. The light is made to pass through a filter.   16. He was seen to be teasing the dog with a bone.

應用練習

PART 1

1. are forbidden; is being repainted   2. are packed; are being loaded

3. is written; are composed; are being selected   4. is not being used; is being repaired

5. are imported; are distributed; are being made   6. is sued; is involved   7. is expected; is completed

8. am being followed; is wanted   9. is placed; is being cut; are being diverted

10. are being arranged; are invited   11. are being made; are being brought; is being leveled

12. is parked; is being measured   13. is being towed

14. are being interrogated; are being held; is arranged   15. is; watched; is; presented

16. are being interviewed; are given   17. is scheduled; is expected   18. are not occupied; are not issued

PART 2

1. The guards have been informed to watch the gate closely.   2. She was shown into a large hall.   3. The dried grass is used as fertilizer.   4. Something must be done for these poor children.   5. The gates are locked every night.   6. The old building is being pulled down.   7. The film must not be exposed to sunlight.   8. The district officer should be informed about the state of affairs here.   9. Were you told to keep it a secret?   10. The bunches of oil-palm fruit are carried to the waiting truck.   11. Why wasn't I told about the change of plans?   12. Far more money is spent on food than on any other thing.   13. These things ought to be kept out of children's reach.   14. Nothing more about the matter will be said if the stolen jewels are returned.   15. Dogs were used to track down the escaped criminals.   16. An enormous dam had been built to keep back the water.   17. Nothing can be done to help you if you don't cooperate.

PART 3

1. He was given an injection and some pills by the doctor./An injection and some pills were given to him by the doctor.   2. He was struck down by a blow on the chin.   3. Has a large part of the building been destroyed by the fire?   4. The poem couldn't have been written by Byron.   5. The new State Secretariat had been opened by the Governor.   6. The answers must be written on one side of the paper only.   7. It can be told that these two letters were written by the same person.   8. A big battle was fought here many years ago.   9. Was the manager impressed by his manner?   10. He was attracted by the large reward.   11. You will be admired for your courage and determination.   12. The room was lit

up for a second by a flash of lightning.   13. The shot was succeeded by complete silence.   14. This question can never be answered satisfactorily.   15. These shells were worn as a protection against evil spirits.   16. A lot of men would be rendered jobless by the closure of the factory.   17. The tubing will be broken by a slight increase in pressure.   18. The lock has been opened and all the money has been taken out.   19. I am told that he had been sentenced to five years in jail by the judge.   20. You cannot be pronounced guilty until it has been proved that you are.

PART 4

1. The figures should be checked carefully.   2. A wallet and some important documents were found near the bus stop.   3. The refrigerator is used to keep vegetables and fruit cool and fresh.   4. He has never been beaten in archery.   5. The film star is being requested to sign some autographs right now.   6. The man was praised by the police chief himself for catching the thief.   7. America was discovered by an Italian named Christopher Columbus.   8. All the furniture will be dusted before the house is swept.   9. The door had certainly been locked when they left the house this morning.   10. The village should not have been built on the riverbank. When the river floods, the village will be swept away.   11. The huge tree was struck and sent toppling down on the house by lightning.   12. Their house was rebuilt, and they were helped out with gifts of food, clothes and furniture by their neighbors.   13. The place has been made dirty by the swallows. Their nests are removed and the place is cleaned up.   14. It was said that the girl was missing/The girl was said to be missing, so a search party was organized. She was found lying unconscious in a deep ditch and was brought home.

PART 5

1. Some top-secret documents were stolen from the Secretariat.   2. The building has not been used for the last fifty years.   3. This incident will be forgotten in a few years' time.   4. He has never been taken at his word.   5. The joke must not be taken too seriously.   6. Her leg was hurt in the match.   7. A bitter battle was fought here years ago.   8. They were told to go away.   9. The bunting should be hung up before the carnival starts.   10. The prisoners were taken away in a van.   11. The traffic regulations must be obeyed.   12. She was asked to finish the work.   13. Football is played in all parts of the world.   14. The truth about the situation will not be revealed.   15. The jewels had not been touched.   16. Will the cattle be rounded up?   17. By whom can this broken chair be repaired?   18. You will be laughed at for asking such a question.   19. You will be thought foolish./It will be thought that you are foolish.   20. Will the visitors be shown around the garden?

PART 6

1. The dog was run over by a truck.　2. The lights were switched off.　3. Was a solution to the problem found?　4. The chair has been made very well by the blind man.　5. The window was closed by an unseen hand.　6. This lovely piece of music was composed by Beethoven.　7. What was being loaded on to the truck?　8. Women are still denied the right to vote in some countries.　9. Were you frightened by the uproar?　10. The frail boat was overturned by a gigantic wave.　11. I shouldn't be treated as if I were a child!　12. The chest has been locked, and it can't be opened.　13. Weren't you told to be here by three o'clock ?　14. The thief was given a fair trial and sent to prison for two years by the judge.　15. I was deeply affected by her misery.

PART 7

1. English is spoken all over the world.　2. This scandal will be forgotten in time to come.　3. This machine can be easily repaired.　4. This parcel was left here for you.　5. Has the room been cleaned yet?　6. We were not told anything about the change of venue.　7. The prisoners were ordered to turn to face the wall.　8. This carpet was made in Iran .　9. The portrait was painted beautifully.　10. You will be taken to the manager's office.　11. This road should be repaired as soon as possible.　12. The girl is being asked to show her passport.　13. The estate was made over to the orphanage.　14. This statement will be taken to be the truth.　15. The spilled milk was licked up by the cat.

PART 8

1. A party was held to celebrate their victory.　2. Many houses were destroyed by the fire.　3. The blind man will be led across the street.　4. Why hasn't anything been done about this matter?　5. Their essays will be handed in tomorrow.　6. That doctor is always spoken well of.　7. What questions were you asked by the interviewer?　8. The criminal has been tracked down by the police. 9. The boy was asked to do a very difficult task.　10. We were shown to our table by the headwaiter himself.　11. A new president of the club will be elected.　12. The door can't be shut properly.　13. John was beaten by Jack in the 100-meter race.　14. The book has been misplaced. It can't be found anywhere.　15. The *Mona Lisa* was painted by Leonardo da Vinci.　16. I was told that your house had been broken into.

PART 9

1. It is believed by the natives that illnesses are caused by evil spirits.　2. It is believed that there are many horizons man can explore.　3. It is feared that all the passengers in the ship were drowned.　4. It is said that there is great potential wealth in the oceans.　5. It was assumed that the answer was correct.　6. It is known that she is innocent of the crime.　7. It was considered that he was the most

brilliant of all the men there.   8. It was claimed that their car was damaged in the accident.   9. It is feared that the Third World War will break out in this generation.   10. It was known that the thief always struck at night.   11. It is thought that the rite is out-dated.   12. It is understood that speeding is an offence.   13. It is believed that there are no sea-serpents in Loch Ness.   14. It is feared that there will be a famine soon.

PART 10

1. It is assumed that the answer is wrong.   2. It is claimed that the country is neutral.   3. It is said that there is a way to make artificial grass.   4. It is said that she had nothing left to live for.   5. It was declared that she was the winner of the competition.   6. It is said that human beings are able to live on food capsules.   7. It is prophesied that there will be a Third World War.   8. It is no longer thought that women have to stay at home.   9. It is believed that the house is haunted.   10. It is considered that this dispute is a matter of personal prejudice.   11. It is known that he is responsible for causing all the trouble.   12. It was assumed that there were no hitches in their plan.   13. It is believed that there is an afterworld.   14. It is claimed that there is a nuclear center on the remote island.

PART 11

1. Money is generally believed to bring happiness.   2. You are not expected to do it alone.   3. A cat is said to have nine lives.   4. They were claimed to be the winners.   5. The country is considered to be the most developed in Asia.   6. The boats are feared to be lost at sea.   7. Bribery is understood to be a crime.   8. He is considered to be the best captain that they ever had.   9. The moon is no longer said to be unconquerable.   10. The other method was considered to be a better one.   11. The white men were believed to have come from the moon by the ignorant natives.   12. She was known to be a dedicated social worker.   13. He was said to be the most generous man in the village.   14. Shakespeare is said to be the greatest poet of all time.   15. He was thought to be a brilliant scientist.   16. She is believed to be telling the truth.   17. He was assumed to have eaten his dinner.   18. A bird in the hand is said to be worth two in the bush.

PART 12

1. The wishing well is believed to have magical powers.   2. The machine was claimed to be able to do the work of twenty men.   3. The project is said to have used up a large amount of money.   4. He is considered to be the most eligible bachelor in town.   5. It is generally assumed that money can buy most things.   6. He is suspected to have taken part in the robbery.   7. He is believed to be the sole heir to the large fortune.   8. Smoking is said to cause lung cancer.   9. The telegram is assumed to

have reached the recipients. 10. The lion is considered to be the king of the beasts. 11. The examination is understood to be of vital importance to him. 12. He is believed to have some special knowledge which can help solve the case. 13. The rocket is said to have circled four times around the moon. 14. Most of the houses are feared to have been washed away by the floodwaters. 15. Spirits of the dead are believed to be gathered in a place called "The Green Pastures." 16. This herb is thought to be a wonderful cure for coughs and colds. 17. The temperature is assumed to remain constant throughout the experiment.

PART 13

1. It is said that there is plenty of food in the oceans. 2. It was known that there are no tigers in Africa. 3. It was supposed that the rats made those nests. 4. It is hoped that all the races live in harmony together. 5. It is feared that there is a time bomb on the plane. 6. It is known that drastic changes have been made in the government. 7. It is no longer thought that the world is flat. 8. It is considered that this issue is a matter of great importance. 9. It is feared that there will be a shortage of food in the near future. 10. It is generally assumed that money is the root of all evil. 11. It is believed that he is guilty of the crime. 12. It is claimed that there will be an earthquake in Tokyo this week.

PART 14

1. He was attacked by the bees when their nest was accidentally disturbed by him. 2. Ink has been spilt all over the floor. The floor must be washed at once. 3. My father has been made the secretary of the Rotary Club. 4. Has the milkman been paid yet? 5. The typewriter has been broken, and it can't be used anymore. 6. The lighted candles and the flowers were left on the altar. 7. I was very much upset by her unkind remarks about my paintings. 8. The car was pushed into the river so that it would not be discovered. 9. It is believed that there will not be any changes in the timetable for the examination. 10. A speech is going to be delivered by the chairman at the annual dinner. 11. While she was being shown around the house, I went out into the garden. 12. He was considered to be an evil man by the villagers. 13. Mr. Baker was praised by the director himself for his thirty years of valuable service to the company. 14. This type of web is made by a poisonous type of spider. 15. It will be kept as a secret if they are paid the money/if the money is paid to them. 16. These words were written by an unknown poet, and they were set to music by someone else. 17. That girl was blamed for bringing bad luck to the village, and she was chased out of the district. 18. The lady was impressed very much by the little boy's courage and determination. 19. The appointment had been made before they were invited for dinner by someone else. 20. He was regarded as a hero by the people in his hometown,

and he was welcomed back with open arms.

Chapter 12 解答

12–1 小練習（本大題的 will 並非唯一標準答案，亦可視情境使用 may、can 等助動詞）

1. will buy　2. are　3. learn　4. won't heal　5. will; promise　6. cries; is　7. entertain

8. will play; lend　9. won't breed　10. won't accept　11. stands　12. will catch　13. won't feel

14. will die

12–2 小練習（本大題的 would 並非唯一標準答案，亦可視情境使用 might、could 等助動詞）

1. Would; climb　2. didn't come　3. would break　4. were; would build　5. were　6. caught

7. went; would find　8. made; would lose　9. would go　10. would withdraw; apologized

11. were; wouldn't accept　12. would agree; allowed　13. broke; would make　14. were sent

應用練習

PART 1（本大題的 will 並非唯一標準答案，亦可視情境使用 may、can 等助動詞）

1. will be　2. clears　3. won't let　4. won't accept　5. becomes　6. Will; promise　7. comes

8. rises　9. agree　10. switch　11. continues　12. won't help　13. rises　14. will happen　15. bring

16. will give　17. won't let　18. Don't give　19. will wait　20. won't believe　21. want

22. doesn't return　23. don't answer　24. will keep

PART 2（本大題的 will 並非唯一標準答案，亦可視情境使用 may、can 等助動詞）

1. will get　2. will break　3. will help　4. will start　5. won't wait　6. will be　7. will stop

8. will meet　9. will bark　10. will remember　11. will go　12. will talk　13. will; take

14. will be flooded　15. will sell　16. will grow　17. Will; believe　18. won't let

PART 3（本大題的 will 並非唯一標準答案，亦可視情境使用 may、can 等助動詞）

1. expand　2. will overflow　3. want　4. strikes　5. rings　6. will agree　7. can assist

8. miss　9. will be　10. give　11. will change　12. thinks　13. will happen　14. promise

15. will; find　16. carry　17. sees　18. will go　19. wait　20. doesn't like

PART 4（本大題的 would 並非唯一標準答案，亦可視情境使用 might、could 等助動詞）

1. would have been　2. had asked　3. hadn't seen　4. would have been; had burned

5. would have bought; had measured　6. would have dried　7. had had

8. hadn't given; would have scolded　9. would have bitten　10. had fallen; would have broken

11. had given　12. hadn't eaten

PART 5（本大題的 will 或 would 並非唯一標準答案，亦可視情境使用 may、can 或 might、could

等助動詞）

1. would hurt　　2. will spoil　　3. would get　　4. starts　　5. would lend　　6. would report

7. would; do　　8. will realize　　9. will; tell　　10. followed　　11. were　　12. wouldn't know　　13. gave

14. didn't accept　　15. dropped　　16. were　　17. would have　　18. failed　　19. will be　　20. practiced

21. would damage　　22. require　　23. wouldn't catch　　24. doesn't shine

PART 6（本大題的 would 並非唯一標準答案，亦可視情境使用 might、could 等助動詞）

1. would have gone　　2. had had　　3. had been　　4. hadn't moved　　5. would have heard

6. wouldn't have gotten　　7. hadn't jumped　　8. had taken　　9. wouldn't have lost

10. would have dropped　　11. wouldn't have escaped　　12. had had　　13. had known

14. wouldn't have been delayed　　15. had brought　　16. would; have done　　17. had worked

18. Would; have rescued

PART 7（本大題的 will 或 would 並非唯一標準答案，亦可視情境使用 may、can 或 might、could 等助動詞）

1. will hear　　2. saw　　3. sprayed　　4. will play　　5. try　　6. would show　　7. were

8. will be injured　　9. pulled　　10. would bear　　11. Would; have bought　　12. won't sell

13. hadn't been　　14. had driven　　15. Would; have waded　　16. will start

PART 8（本大題的 will 或 would 並非唯一標準答案，亦可視情境使用 may、can 或 might、could 等助動詞）

1. would have gone　　2. had realized　　3. is　　4. would deliver　　5. wouldn't know

6. would make　　7. would; do　　8. would have recovered　　9. call　　10. will believe　　11. won't tell

12. would be allowed　　13. continues　　14. hadn't wound　　15. were　　16. were

17. would have answered　　18. keep　　19. wouldn't have suspected　　20. wouldn't call

English Grammar Juncture

英文文法階梯

康雅蘭 嚴雅貞　編著

專為想要重新學好文法的讀者
所編寫的初級文法教材

- 一網打盡高中職各家版本英文課程所要求的文法基礎，為往後的英語學習打下良好基礎。

- 盡量以句型呈現文法，避免冗長解說，配上簡單易懂的例句，讓學習者在最短時間內掌握重點，建立整體架構。

- 除高中職學生外，也適合讓想要重新自修英文文法的讀者溫故知新之用。

Practical English Grammar

實用英文文法（完整版）

馬洵 劉紅英 郭立穎　編著
龔慧懿　編審

專為大專學生及在職人士學習英語所編寫的實用文法教材

- 涵蓋英文文法、詞彙分類、句子結構及常用句型。
- 凸顯實用英文文法，定義力求簡明扼要，以圖表條列方式歸納文法重點，概念一目了然。
- 搭配大量例句，情境兼具普遍與專業性，中文翻譯對照，方便自我進修學習。

實用英文文法實戰題本

馬洵 劉紅英　編著

- 完全依據《實用英文文法》出題，實際活用文法概念。
- 試題數量充足，題型涵蓋廣泛，內容符合不同程度讀者需求。
- 除每章的練習題外，另有九回綜合複習試題，加強學習效果。
- 搭配詳盡試題解析本，即時釐清文法學習要點。

Cloze & Writing Practice

克漏字與寫作練習（全新改版）

李文玲　編著

考場克敵制勝，教您「寫」脈賁張！
克漏字與寫作的完美組合，橫掃大小考試的終極利器！
30篇克漏字短文精心設計：
Basic 18篇—指導基礎句型寫作
Advanced 12篇—傳授進階作文技巧

You Can Write!

寫作導引（全新改版）

李文玲　編著

大家一起來「寫」拼
1. 從寫作概念的介紹到各種文體的寫作策略，循序漸進。
2. 近百題的實戰演練。
3. 每章另闢小單元，分享寫作的小技巧與常面臨的問題。